Dead in the Water

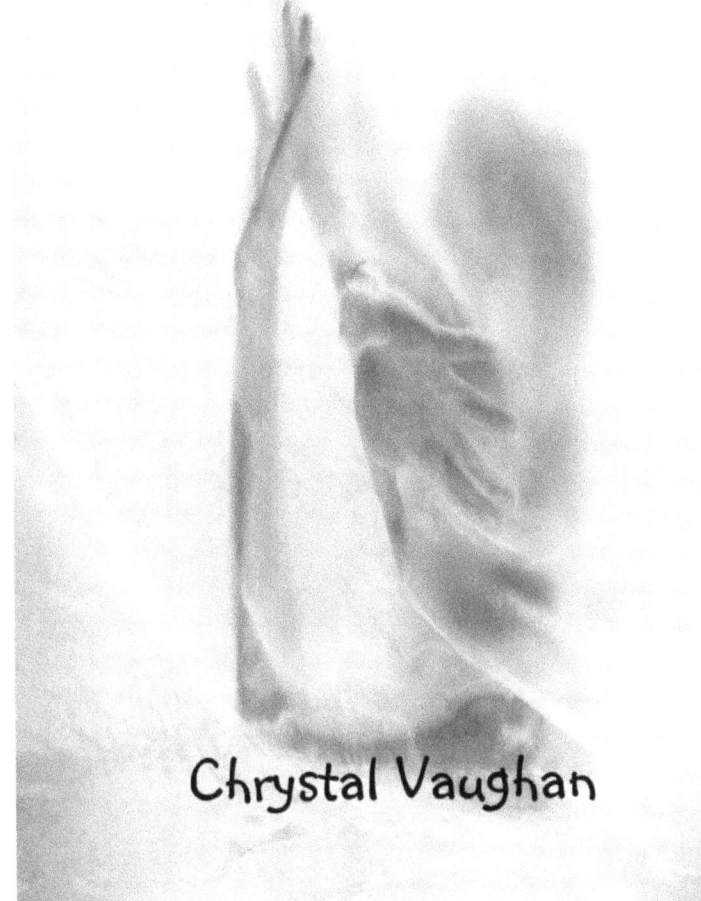

Chrystal Vaughan

Dead in the Water

By
Chrystal Vaughan

Cover Art:
Michelle Crocker

http://mlcdesigns4you.weebly.com/

Publisher's Note:

This is a work of fiction. All names, characters, places, and
events are the work of the author's imagination.

Any resemblance to real persons, places, or events is
coincidental.

Solstice Publishing - www.solsticepublishing.com

Dedicated to Emily Valentine and the Judith Kids.
Judith loves ya.

Other works by Chrystal Vaughan:
Sideshow

Eva

September 15, 2013

I'm starting journal number one in the series I like to call "Evalyn Dunbar: The Weird Chronicles." I decided to start writing in a journal for myself so I don't expect anyone to read it but I want to, like, look back through them and laugh at what a dork I was. Am.

But in case someone does read it, in the event I'm dead or something, I'm Evalyn Dunbar (duh) and I spend most of my time being alone. That's because of how strange I am. My mom says words like "unique" and "different" and my dad doesn't say anything, he just pretends I'm normal. He's even weirder than me.

Being sixteen sucks the big one. Today in chemistry class, Jesse Williams started to come sit by me at the lab table but stupid, Barbie, slutbag Natasha Milligan tossed her blond locks and saggy boobs in his direction and he went over to her table instead, slavering like the dog he is. He did smile back at me like in apology, but I don't care. Jesse used to be my best friend back in grade school but ever since about sixth grade, right before junior high, he's been a real jerk.

Jesse's mom and my mom have been best friends since they were little kids. In this town (that's Brookings, Oregon to be exact) people come here and stay forever. There is no escaping. So Jess and me were doomed to be friends since we were born. Which had been a great fate up until it wasn't anymore.

So that was just the start to my rotten day. It only gets worse when you're Eva Dunbar. The kids used to call me Evil Dumbear when I was younger, but then they started being afraid of me. Now they strive for indifference. It's pathetic, really.

I read online that I'm supposed to write a description of myself in any journal-type thing. Ok fine, here goes. I spend a lot of time online because I'm by myself up in my room, but mostly I read, write, and draw. Also, I'm sixteen, as I said, I have medium-length black hair, regular blue eyes (instead of piercing, pale, dreamy, or any other lame adjective), pale skin because I never go outside, and I'm like a stick figure so I'll never have any boobs or a butt. I like to wear oversized sweaters, hoodies, and jeans. Um, and I'm a spirit writer. I guess that covers it. I'll write more tomorrow.

Jesse

Jesse watched Eva's eyes darken with hatred as she stared daggers at Natasha. He wanted to think it was because she was jealous but she never talked to him anymore so he doubted it. There was just something about Natasha that Eva had always hated, since they were all in grade school together. He tuned out Natasha's nasal voice, bitching about Eva, and watched as Eva studiously ignored him, like she'd turn to stone if she looked in his general direction. Her rich, black hair curved down her pale cheek and over her delicate shoulder, hidden as it was under thick layers of hoodie material. Jesse sighed and turned back to the lesson. If he failed chemistry, his parents would take away his Jeep and he'd be forced to take the bus to school and work.

He had good intentions but his mind drifted back to when he and Eva had been inseparable. There was a time when he thought he was in love with her. Scratch that, he had known it. Eva was all he could think about. His brother Aaron finally grew tired of his mooning about, over her, and told him he should "hit that and get over it" which, to his dismay, sounded half wonderful; the hitting it part. He envisioned a future with Eva though, not just a moment, and at twelve the idea kind of scared him, both the sex and the future. In confusion, he'd backed off of spending time with her and kept to himself for a while. Now, five years later, he could see in hindsight that what he'd done was stupid but he didn't know how to fix it, other than playing childish games like trying to make her jealous with hoes like Natasha. He never did seem to get a break, a time to talk to her alone, and he was too embarrassed to go to her house, facing not only her on her own turf, but also her parents who he saw on a regular basis at his house. He avoided them, too. He could tell they were puzzled why he wasn't a friend with their daughter anymore, just like his parents were. But what could he tell them?

Jesse sighed. Natasha was whining that he didn't listen to her. She was so freaking annoying. Natasha was one of those girls who thought her boobs and her willingness to put out were all a guy needed in a girl; that, and the occasional bottle of rum from her dad's liquor cabinet. Maybe it worked on most guys; hell, it must have if all the guys in the locker room were telling the truth. Of course, she had told him a little bit about what went on in her life, in her house. He kind of felt sorry for her, but not sorry enough to listen to her jabbering.

Mr. Riggs, the chemistry teacher, was still going on about the periodic table of elements and alkali metals. Jesse began to feel as though this day would never end.

Eva

September 18, 2013

So I didn't write more tomorrow. I mean yesterday, or whenever it was. Sue me. I was busy with something else. Here is where I have to tell you, nonexistent reader, about what it is that's wrong with me. I have this thing that happens where I can be drawing or writing a poem or whatever angst-y, teenage crap I'm doing at the moment, and something sort of takes over my hands and my brain goes on vacation. I don't remember these "episodes" as my mom calls them but when I come back to myself, there's like some new writing or drawing on the paper. That's why I write and draw so much. It's never fun to have one of these things hit me when I don't have any paper. So I'm always carrying around a notebook and pens like a complete nerd.

When I was really little, like one year old, my mom gave me a box of those giant crayons. You know the ones, the super huge ones like toilet paper rolls in your chubby little fists? Anyway, then she taped butcher paper on the floor in our kitchen and I went to town. I don't, of course, remember any of that stuff. But it must have freaked her the hell out the first time I started writing or drawing something from somewhere else. She doesn't like to talk about it, but I've eavesdropped enough to know that it was a scary picture of a guy cutting off another guy's head with some kind of machete or sword or something.

After that first time, I went to the doctor a lot. My parents must have thought I was born to be a serial killer. Anyway, the doctor said I was fine but then it happened again. Only this time, I was drawing on my butcher-paper floor and my dad saw me have a spirit-writing episode. Pretty creepy I bet. I ended up writing a suicide note from some boy named Rodney Gaines. It was signed and everything, even though I was only a little kid and couldn't even spell my own name.

Anyways, they took me to more doctors, and more doctors. Funny how the writing stuff never happened in a doctor's office. I guess people don't die very often in there. I've never been to a hospital but I have a feeling that would be a bad idea. The doctors didn't suppose I have like multiple personalities or something. I guess I did all their stupid puzzles correctly. They kind of just shrugged it off and my parents gave up on the magic of modern medicine to fix me. They just made arrangements with my school to be able to have me go to the nurse's office if it happens there. It has, twice; that's why kids are scared of me. They think I'm a freak, and it's catching, or something. Idiots. They don't totally know what happens because the teachers have all been warned about my "epileptic seizures" and the warning signs, and they are all quick to shuttle me out of the room until it's over only to send me to the nurse and call one of my parents. But the other kids know enough. They seem to know it's something more than a medical condition and they punish me in a million small ways for my difference.

I didn't figure out it was spirit writing until I was older and I got my first cell phone. I was kinda spoiled cuz it was a smart phone and had Internet on it. My parents are pretty clueless about that stuff, so I got to pick, and I got an iPhone. I started researching what was wrong with me and I found this (I have the computer now, so it makes it easier to look crap like this up):

From Wikipedia:
Automatic writing
or **psychography**
is writing, which the
writer claims to be
produced from a
subconscious,
and/or external
and/or spiritual
source without
conscious
awareness of the
content.

I like that, "claims to be." As if I'd do this for fun. Ok, so usually I just hide away the stuff that whatever is using my hand writes or draws, but from now on, I'm going to scan it in and paste it into this journal.

September 22, 2013
Nothing, so far. I think they (whoever 'they' are) are waiting for something. Maybe Halloween. It's usually worse around then. Gotta lotta homework today. Stupid Mr. Clausen gave us Macbeth questions, due by tomorrow. As if the weird girl needs any help dwelling on death. The kids already think I'm a witch or something.

September 23, 2013
No writing, yet. The last time was a picture that came through of a hangman's noose in an attic. But I tucked it away. I don't even tell my parents when it happens anymore because it just stresses them out. No wonder I'm an only child. They didn't want another freaky kid in their house. Can't say I blame them.

Today in chemistry, I tried to think of ways to burn off Natasha's hair so she wouldn't be so freaking smug anymore, every time Jesse sits with her. Unfortunately, I'm failing chemistry so I wasn't able to come up with anything.

September 28, 2013
This is what I wrote last night, or what something wrote using my hand. I scanned it in to keep the scratchy handwriting.

drowning

So evidently something wants me to drown. Or something is drowning; I'm not sure which. This kind of thing used to really scare me but I'm sort of use to it now. I don't know what this means or what, if anything, I'm supposed to do about it. I don't swim, so I'm safe on that score, and I take showers not baths so...whatever you are, if you're like reading over my shoulder, can you maybe give me a hint? I'm not good with this esoteric crap.

October 2, 2013
Worst day, ever; gym class was ridiculous. I hate dressing down for gym and the jerk-wad gym teacher, Mrs. McGhee, made me take my hoodie off. All the girls were making fun of my pasty, scrawny legs and arms. I had to throw my hair up in a knot on top of my head because she made us run laps around the gym and it was hotter than hell in there. I don't know why we couldn't go outside. It was fall for gods sake, not the dead of winter. The precious delicate flowers won't die of frostbite. I swear if there ever was a zombie apocalypse, I would come back here and

12

bite off McGhee's head as my first act of the newly reanimated. To top it off, I keep finding notes in my locker with quotes from the witches in Macbeth on them. I wish I was a witch. I'd catch those losers and make them sorry.

I still don't know what the word 'drowning' was supposed to mean. Usually I don't care; I just stack up the papers with the words or drawings on them and hide them in a box under my bed. But I was reading where some people actually try to do this kind of thing on purpose (*idiots*) and then figure out how they can help the spirits or ghosts or whatever these things are. Maybe if I do that, they'll help me out? I don't know. I'm just tired of being tired of my freakiness. I'm like a Goth girl without even meaning to be. I'd give anything for tanned skin, blond hair, and curves. Or friends.

October 16, 2013

Been super busy with school. Oh, and guess what? Jesse Williams came over to my HOUSE! I was blown away. Of course, he did get stuck on the same learning team with me in English class so that's why he came over; for schoolwork. But it was just the two of us, and my parents weren't home thank god. I, of course, looked like crap. He came over last Saturday afternoon and I was still in my pajama pants and ever-present hoodie. I hadn't even brushed my hair or my teeth and I was totally depressed. The night before, when I was trying to read the new Neil Gaiman book, I came to myself a while later and found my notebook open on my bed and this drawn in it:

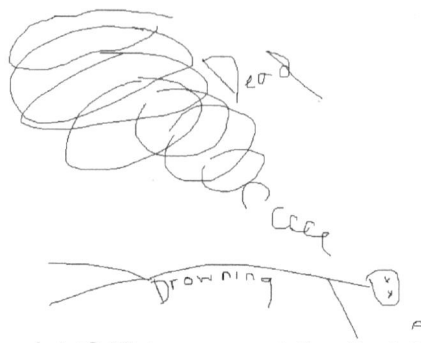

Cheery right? This was not the first time I've had a recurring theme, unfortunately. Another time, I had the same word show up on my notebook for like weeks. It just said "BALLS" over and over again in really heavy black printing. I figured it was the spirit of some pervert.

This one was really fun with the whole drowning thing. NOT. I understand dead and drowning, whatever you are. I'm curious what the little mark is in the corner under the head with no nose and mouth, and the swirly tornado thing is really weird.

Ok but back to Jesse coming over. So I'm a total mess right, but he's all perfect and blond and tall and sexy. I swear high school boys shouldn't be allowed to have muscles and look like movie stars, especially around freaky girls like me. It's just inhumane. He's standing there all-delicious and I'm like, "Hey, Jesse, what are you doing here?" like a total jerk. And he just smiles at me with perfect white TV commercial teeth and he's like, "Hey, Eva, you want to get started on our MacBeth questions?" Because our sadistic English teacher Clausen has decided we have to write our own questions for the horror that was MacBeth. So I muttered something intelligent like, "yeah sure whatever," and turned around and went inside the house.

Jesse followed me inside and we went up to

14

my room. He's been to my house a million times before but never since we started high school so it was kind of strange. I wonder how different it looks to him, and he must have been thinking the same thing because he asked why the stairway walls were painted blue now instead of pink. I paused on the stairs and just kind of gave him a blank look. Why the hell would they still be pink? Did he think I was still eleven years old? He sorta blushed and stopped asking questions about my décor. I'd actually lobbied to get them painted black to match my mood swings but my parents refused.

So we got up to my room and it was totally trashed. I'm all embarrassed and I started throwing clothes and books and crap into a corner, when he came up next to me and started helping. He actually grabbed one of my bras with a pile of clothes before I could stop him! I was mortified. Not that my bras are anything to brag about but jeez I don't want Mr. Tall, Hot, and Blond to be touching my undies. For the second time in two minutes, he was blushing again.

I hadn't put my notebook away from the night before and it was still lying open on my bed. I made a dive for it but his long arms passed right by me and snatched it up. It was suddenly like we were ten again, with him holding my notebook up in the air and me jumping around wildly like a freaking Chihuahua trying to grab it from him. I lunged upward to make a final desperate grab for it, but ended up throwing myself into him and sliding full length down his side, and that whole nostalgic childhood feeling was gone in an instant. He caught me by my waist to steady me, and held me pressed against his side for the longest time; it felt like. I have read those trashy romance books where the boy and girl stare deep into each other's eyes, but never in a gazillion years would I

15

have imagined it happening to me, with Jesse Williams of all people. He arched a perfect eyebrow at me and I let my arms fall from where they'd landed, clasped around his neck. I'm pretty sure I was the only one blushing by that point.

I pushed myself away from him like he was suddenly a poisonous snake with three heads and just kind of stood awkwardly in the middle of my bedroom. It sort of seemed like a bad idea to have him there, at that moment, but there wasn't anything I could do about it now.

He still had my notebook. I waited patiently while he thumbed rapidly through its pages in a shocking display of disregard for *other people's privacy*, as if he hadn't stopped coming over years ago, and had the right to help himself to my stuff.

So he's looking through these pictures and I'm thinking he probably assumes I'm just the strangest person ever, and the worst artist, too, cause those pictures are kind of preschool-ish. But hey, if you were dead and had to use some living girl's hands, a girl who actually can't really draw either, then they're pretty damn good considering those little restrictions. Jess goes, "Eva this is really disturbing. Why do you write this kind of stuff?"

"Jeez, Jesse, why don't you mind your own business? I guess I can write or draw whatever I want. You're not the art police." What a witty comeback, right?

"I just worry about you. You don't talk to anyone at school. You cover up in giant clothes all the time, and you hide behind your hair. You don't even come sit with me at lunch or anything. And now this...drawing."

What? Ok so we were going to do this right now. Fine. "You know what, Jesse? I don't think I can do homework with you today, or ever. I'm going to ask to be switched off your team."

"What the hell would you do that for?" he demanded.

"Because you freaking jerk, you can't just stop being my friend and then be all but hurt when I don't come chasing after you to talk to me!"

"I never stopped being your friend! You got weirder and weirder and shut me out of your life!" he yelled at me, really loud at the top of his lungs. It completely startled me and I took a closer look at him. He was pale, and shaking, with two red blotches high on his cheeks. That's what he looked like when he was really super angry, always had been since we'd known each other. Like from birth. I all of the sudden realized that his mom must not have told him anything about my problem. Was that possible? She hadn't blabbed? I know that she knows, her and my mom are thick as thieves. But she kept it from Jesse; why?

There he was, this kid that use to be my best friend, just standing there in the middle of my room breathing hard and glaring at me, one hand gripping my notebook and the other curled into a fist at his side. He looked like he wanted to deck me. I took a deep breath and stepped closer to him, looking up at his angry face. And then I did something really stupid. I said, "You want to know, Jesse? You really want to know why I am this way?"

He didn't say anything for a long time but that pissed off look started to drain off and was unfortunately replaced with something closer to determination. "I have been waiting for so long for you to let me in, Eva." Shit.

Dammit! I gotta go, my mom is calling me down for dinner. I'll write down the rest later.

October 18, 2013

    There's been another "drowning" in my notebook. Here it is.

October 20, 2013

    I have been so depressed lately. I can barely drag myself out of bed. But I was thinking I'd better finish writing what happened when Jesse was at my house the other day. Before I was so rudely interrupted by my mother's lasagna.

    After we stared at each other for a while, it occurred to me how freaking tall he was so I turned and sat cross legged on my bed, hugging my pillow to my stomach and curling over it like a giant prawn. He came and sat down next to me, kinda perched on the edge of my bed, and we didn't say anything for a long time. I finally grabbed my notebook from his hand, and opened it to the front page, and handed it back to him. "Read from the beginning, every page, in order."

    I watched him thoroughly inspect the pages, his brows all furrowed up in concentration. It was so cute, really; he still has that line that goes down through the center of his eyebrows when he's concentrating super hard. He reads really fast too; I watched his eyes scan back and forth through the words and pages with incredible speed. I mean, it's not the same as this electronic journal, it's all drawings and words from whoever uses me to channel their stuff, but it's still a whole notebook full of stuff.

In much less time than it would have taken me, he was done. He closed my notebook and laid it gently on the bed next to him, and then he just stared down at his clasped hands, his head kind of hanging down. That stupid part of my brain started whispering things like, *now he knows what a freak you are* and *he'll never speak to you again*, so I of course had to say something. Did I mention that I read a lot? I know that what I did next is called a preemptive strike.

"Now that you know, you don't have to worry about me trying to be friends with you. I won't interfere in your perfect life."

"How long, Eva? How long have you been writing these things?"

"Hey genius, I don't write them. It's called spirit writing, ok? There's something wrong with me, where someone or something, some DEAD thing, can just use my hands and brain to write or draw whatever they want!" I'm practically shouting at this point and his astonished look is sort of worth it. "And there isn't SHIT I can do about it! It's like a trance. You get it? I have no idea it's happened until I sort of wake back up and there it is. And it's happened to me my entire life! Not that you would know anything about my life the past several years, right?"

I wasn't really prepared for what happened next; I guess I was expecting him to just leave. But instead he turned to me and, faster than I've ever seen a human move, he grabbed my pillow, flung it away and wrapped his arms around me, dragging me onto his lap and holding me really tight. Naturally, I struggled to get away because I'm a complete idiot.

After all, it wasn't as though my childhood friend turned complete hunk was hugging me, or anything. Eva Dunbar…genius.

But he didn't let me go. He just waited; hanging on with those iron arms, until I wore myself out which wasn't long. Clearly, I don't spend as much time in the gym as he does. But then the worst thing happened. I finally lay there all limp and exhausted in his arms, and he pulled me closer, and whispered, "Why didn't you tell me sooner? You shouldn't have had to go through all this by yourself."

Cue Eva, the Queen of the Waterworks. I swear it was the most embarrassing thing. I'm just sitting there crying like a freaking baby, getting his (probably) expensive shirt all wet with my tears and snot. And then I got mad. Because when I cry, I get mad. How dare he feel sorry for me? How dare he make me cry? I was handling all this shit just fine without his help! And he was the one who stopped coming over! *He* left *me*! So I got really pissed and pushed him away. I stood over him, looking at his shocked face, and yelled and screamed at him about how he had abandoned me so how could I tell him, and I didn't need him to save and protect me, and a bunch of other really mean things I'm ashamed of and can't write down. Basically, I threw some books at him and ran him out of my house. I might have even told him that I didn't like him. I thought he was an asshole, and he should go crawling back to that slut, whore, Natasha, who obviously thinks the sun shines out of his ass, or something like that. God, I wished I were dead right now. I wish that a lot.

Jesse

Jesse was elated when the English teacher paired him up with Eva on the Learning Teams for MacBeth. The two other team members were buddies of his, so he quickly outlined a plan for the team. "Me and Eva will take the first ten questions. You guys can take the last ten, and then give them all to me and I'll put them together, with Eva's help." Everyone nodded except Eva. "Is that ok, Ev?" "Fine," she mumbled. Jesse frowned. Not exactly the cheery response he'd hoped for but he'd take it. At least she said something to him. God, how he missed her.

He decided to go over to her house a few days after the assignment had been given, to go over their parts and maybe study together; any excuse to be near her, really. He wanted nothing more than to find excuses to touch her soft skin, give her a hug and feel her fragile bones under his arms and protect them with his strength, or to smell the coconut shampoo scent of her rich, dark hair. Anything.

He drove his Jeep over to her house, and the route from his house to her house felt like deja vu. He'd gone there so many times, back and forth from house to house, but not for the last few years. He noticed weeds where there hadn't been before, and new cracks in the sidewalks they used run and ride their bikes on. He felt kind of sad seeing all that decay where once they'd played, happily.

He parked in her driveway, noticing both her parents weren't home. She answered the door wearing a hoodie sweatshirt and a pair of pajama pants, her hair pulled up in a messy bun, looking downright adorable.

He followed her up her stairs to her room,

making some lame comment about the paint. He felt so tongue-tied around her now that he had her to himself, away from school and other people. He had no idea what to say. She started picking up her room when they got there, seeming embarrassed by the mess. She'd always been messy though, maybe she thought he'd forgotten? He tried to help her out, but just made it worse by grabbing a pile of clothes with her bra under it; a very lacy bra, a very pink, skimpy, lacy bra. He might never wash that hand again, he thought.

He finally found some common ground, though, when he spied her notebook on the bed. As a kid, she'd always carried one of these around but when he asked her about it, she said she was just drawing doodles and writing notes in them. He never thought much of it. Girls were different like that, right? Sometimes she'd draw him, playing with the soccer ball or standing on his head, and then show him so he always figured that's what it was. But when he grabbed the one on her bed, she went after him and his natural reaction was to hold it over his head where she couldn't reach it. And it was worth the angry look in her eyes because her action threw her entire body up against his. His whole side tingled where she was pressed up against him, her breast squished against his ribcage and her soft hip pushed into his leg. She was so soft in so many places, and yet he could feel how fragile she was under all that softness. He was sorry when she pushed away from him, like he'd suddenly caught on fire and she was burned or something.

He tried to distract himself, and his body, by flipping through the pages of her notebook. He slowed down, though, as he actually looked closer at what was in there. Page after page of little stick figures with

XX's for eyes, ropes around their necks, or knives sticking out of them. The last few pages had one that had writing on it, where the word "drowning" was scratched in with wobbly handwriting. It wasn't like Eva's normally bubbly handwriting; he knew, because he watched her write in class. Her regular writing was more rounded. He was instantly suspicious. Did she have a boyfriend with a learning disorder that he didn't know about?

His questioning of the notebook contents did not go well, probably because he was trying to hide how suspicious he was. She got pretty mad at him and threatened to have herself switched off their learning team and accused him of abandoning their friendship. Jesse lost his temper.

"I never stopped being your friend! You got weirder and weirder and shut me out of your life!" he shouted at her. He immediately regretted yelling, since it hurt his throat and did nothing to remove that wounded animal look from her eyes. Plus, it wasn't entirely true. The shame of his lie burned his throat with a taste as bitter as bile.

He didn't know how long he could take the silence, until she finally cracked and showed him what she had been hiding from him for all those years. At first, Jesse couldn't believe his eyes. He thought maybe Eva was really mentally disturbed and he nearly excused himself to call his mother and explain how Eva needed help right away. His mom was a nurse, and she'd always helped Eva's parents when she was sick. But then he noticed that the notebook had different types of writing. And some of the pictures were more sophisticated than the others. It was as if different hands had written and drawn these things in the notebooks. He wondered if it could be multiple personality disorder? She claimed the spirits of dead people were using her hands to write these things. She was so earnest, Jesse almost believed her.

He gathered her close to him, just to hold her and let her know she wasn't alone anymore. Eva always hated crying, so he should have known better but God, he didn't know what else to do. He still had all these feelings for her, and they were more intense than ever now that he was in her presence again. But Jesus, she was crazy, wasn't she? She had to be, there was no such thing as ghosts or spirits or spirit writing in Jesse's philosophy.

But there was also no such thing as a world without Eva. Although she had gotten so pissed off at him, he was sure she would never want to see him again. She threw a couple of the books she was reading at his head, and he dodged them easily as he made his way down the stairs, two at a time. He decided to give her a little time. Maybe her story would change if he were patient with her. Then he could get her some help. He felt sorry for the girl who had been his friend, all those years ago.

Eva

October 24, 2013

I feel sick about what I did. None of this was Jesse's fault. I don't know why he stopped coming over but the spirit-writing thing had nothing to do with him. I guess it scares me sometimes, no matter how much I say it doesn't, and I have no one who understands to talk to about it. I took all that out on him and now, when I see him in the hallway at school, I look down really quick and run the other way. I should apologize to him but I'm too much of a coward. I feel like I'm going to puke just writing about it. I just hope he forgets what he read in my notebook and forgets about me completely. That would be the best thing for us both, even though that makes my chest hurt, and I have trouble breathing just thinking about it. I guess that's why I'm so depressed. Also it's almost Halloween, and things are always worse around then. I go for days feeling like my skin is crawling and that something is watching me. And there's always new words or drawings in my book, like I spend more time outside myself than in. I'm dreading it.

School has been relentless, to top off my utterly stupid temper tantrum that drove away the most amazing guy on earth. The teachers are giving us more homework than ever, I haven't even started on my English crap, and people keep messing with my locker. Yesterday, someone wrote "FREAK" on it in black magic marker and even the janitor had a hard time getting it off. I finally had to talk to the principal, Mr. Herron, about it and now they let me carry every single book I have in a ginormous backpack to all my classes. Maybe I'll get some muscles, since I'm not getting any curves.

October 30, 2013

It is so cold here; endless white
Drives madly about my feet.
A swirling blizzard; snowy
And unforgiving.

It is so dark here; seething black
Surrounds cruelly around my neck.
A suffocating madness; void
And unforgiving.

It is so lonely here; expanding grey
Whirls crazily inside my head.
A dizzying vertigo; cloudy
And unforgiving.

It is so empty here; surrounding clear
Follows hungrily around my heart.
A cloying storm; transparent
And unforgiving.

It is so lost here; despairing colors
Clutch eagerly at my soul.
A hopeless wind; damaged
And unforgiving.

October 31, 2013

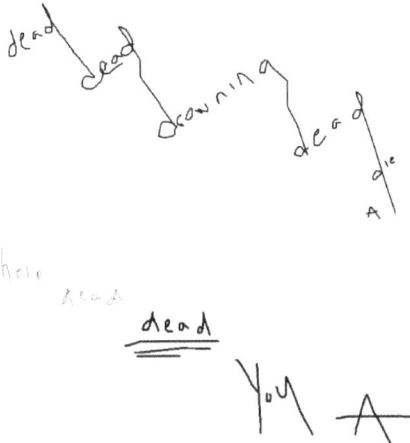

November 1, 2013

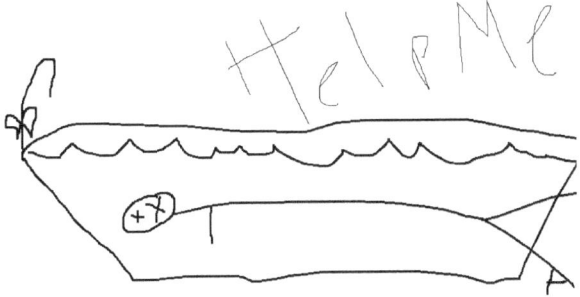

November 2, 2013

November 4, 2013
  I've been in this bed for over a week. I'm never getting out of it. I feel cold all over. No blankets can make me warm ever again. I wish I were dead.

November 8, 2013

Mom made me eat soup. It was so hot. I'm so cold. I've been shivering for days and days. I heard my dad's voice say I should go to the hospital but my mom said it was just a virus, nothing but a virus. Virus. Virus, virus, virus.

November 16, 2013

Tell me how.

help
me

November 18, 2013

That was the worst I've ever felt. Right now I'm sitting up in my bed, for the first time in days. It's never been this bad before. Usually there is a lot more spirit writing in my notebook but this time I was really sick. I'm used to being kind of depressed most of the time. I think that's from being a teenage girl, and oh yes, also a freak. I dunno. But this time I really wanted to kill myself. I got so cold and felt as though I'd never be warm again. There was only four spirit-writing sessions too. I wonder if it was because I was ill. Maybe they can't get through when I'm delirious? A more chilling thought happened when I saw what I'd drawn though. What if I spent more time out of my body, than in it? I've spent most of today scanning the notebook pages into this journal. I don't remember writing much of those posts, but in a normal "hey, I'm sick" kind of way instead of a creepy way. I tried to just put the notebook pictures in where I think they fit best; there were no dates on them in the notebook. Random randomness is thy name, ha-ha.

November 19, 2013

OMG. Jesse just left my house. I have to write down what happened before I forget every amazing second.

So, my mom comes upstairs and checks my forehead and I'm all cranky from being in sweat pants and under blankets for like two weeks. Thank god I took a shower yesterday; after that drawing I can never take a bath again, so thanks for that, who or whatever you are. But the shower felt good on my aching muscles, though it took about an hour to comb out my ratty hair. Anyway, so Mom is checking me out to see if I'm still alive and then she goes, "Do you feel up to company, honey?" and I'm at DEFCON 5 immediately because: a) no one ever comes to see me, and b) she's being all nicey-nice since I was sick. I know that she knows damn good and well what happened aside from the actual virus. But what can either of us do about it? So we pretend as usual that I was only just "sick" and not possessed or whatever happened. Still the over solicitous thing is sort of bizarre. We don't do that in our family. Everyone does pretty much their own thing; like a bunch of roommates or something.

I must have looked pretty suspicious because she says, "Jesse Williams is here to see you," and I freaked the hell out.

"Mom! No, don't let him in here," I basically hissed at her. But it was too late. I saw him coming up the stairs like some glorious Greek god, holding flowers of all things. Mom just smiled at me and patted him on the shoulder as she left. The traitor!

There he was, coming up the stairs with this massive bouquet of stargazer lilies, which are my favorite flowers, and a heart-breaking smile. I'm so rude, I just go, "What are you doing here?" hoping he'll go away. But leave the flowers.

He laid the flowers down gently on my desk, powdering my papers all gold with flower dust, which is beautiful and makes my eyes tear up for some reason. He comes over and sits on the edge of my bed, again, just like last time and I'm sort of panicking inside because the last time he came near me things went horribly wrong and I was terrible to him. Just thinking about that made me feel so bad, I blurted out, "Jesse, I'm really sorry about all that crap I said to you when you were here before." There. That felt good. "But I'm really sick and you should probably go before you catch my cooties or something."

He just smiled at me. His eyes searched my face for something...he must not have found it because his smile faded and he leaned a little closer. His breath was so minty and delicious smelling that it made me a little dizzy. And before I knew it, he was kissing me. His lips were soft, but sort of demanding, which I liked. I closed my eyes, and put my arms around his neck, just like in the movies. His hand reached forward and crept up the back of my head, burying his fingers in my thankfully untangled hair and pulling me closer. He touched my lips with his. Soon we were exploring with tongues and lips until I broke the kiss, gasping for breath. How romantic. I can see the epitaph on my tombstone now: Eva died from her first kiss due to sinus congestion.

He pulled back and studied my face again, that worry line showing up between his eyebrows in the most adorable way. I glared at him, feeling my face go completely red and in true Eva Dunbar fashion, I get all demanding and go, "Why did you do that? Can't you get any of your Barbie hoes to kiss you?"

He sighed and let me go. That was brilliant, Eva, I thought. Way to go. He comes over with flowers and kisses you, and you gotta go ruin it. Maybe a nunnery will take me in, nah, probably not. They don't really like people who are possessed by demons or ghosts or whatever was wrong with me.

"Eva, why do you always have to push me away?"

"I didn't push you away, I was just asking. I know you have a lot of girlfriends." This was said with bitterness, I confess.

"No, I don't. Those girls are just groupies that hang out with my guy friends. I've never gone out with any of them. They follow us around because we are on the sports teams and they think they like us or we like them."

"Really?" Insert my scathing sarcasm here.

"Yes, really. If you would open your eyes, you'd see that."

"What about how every time we are in chemistry class, you go and sit with that stupid, cow Natasha?" HA! Point for me.

"I only sit with her to make you jealous so you'll start talking to me again."

"Oh."

Suddenly he looked pretty cheerful. "Does it work?"

There were two choices here. My defensive side said to tell him hell no, you're not jealous of that bimbo or him either for that matter. My honest side was jumping up and down saying hell yes, it makes me crazy. I choose honesty instead of defensive, for a change. Maybe there's hope for me yet.

"Yes. It works every time. It breaks my heart to

watch you walk away from me…again." There, take some guilt with your honest answer, Jesse Williams. And it worked pretty well, too, because the confessions started pouring out of him like he'd been given a super heavy dose of truth serum.

"I never meant to hurt you. I stopped coming over when we were younger because I started having all these feelings about you. And you started acting really weird and all secretive, like you were hiding something. I thought you didn't like me in the same way. I didn't know what to do. Aaron (that would be Jesse's older brother) said it was because I wanted to…sleep with…you and I should just do it and get it over with, that I'd stop thinking about you all the time if I did. But that's not what I wanted. I was confused, and so I did anything I could to avoid you. And then you just stopped talking to me so I figured that was how you wanted it."

This was both startlingly good and horribly painful. He had told me I was the one who shut him out, but now he was admitting he was wrong, it was his fault. No way was I keeping quiet about this crap. "Well, Jesse, I'm so sorry to have hurt you in such a terrible manner. My god, how have you managed to survive?"

"Goddammit, Eva. You and that smart fucking mouth!" Shocking curse words coming from the high school football god, handsomest Homecoming King ever, and all around good old American golden boy. Golden boy apparently had enough of my smart, effing mouth because he grabbed me by the shoulders and kissed me again. This was way different from our last kiss though. It was more urgent, hotter, more shocking, taking but not giving. It was the most incredible thing that has happened to me in my whole life, as yet. And I can channel the spirits of the dead, so that's saying something.

Jess pressed me back against my covers, still kissing me, but a little more gently now, both hands buried back in my hair and holding my face captive where he wanted me. I wrapped my arms around his broad back and kissed him back with everything I had. All the missing him, all the hurt and anger and fear, I poured those emotions into lust and fed them into his waiting mouth. I could feel him lying on top of me, and I felt a hardness between us, which scared and excited me at the same time. I must have made some sound, because he broke off our kiss and just stared down into my eyes, like he was looking for my soul so he could devour that, too.

"I've never been able to stop thinking about you, you know. I've wanted to come back and be friends if nothing else, for so long, but I was afraid of your temper, afraid you would reject me."

"Well, I guess you had something to fear then. I am kind of a bitch, I guess."

"No. You're honest about your feelings no matter how raw they are. It's one of the things I love about you."

He said love. I heard it. I'm writing it down right here so that if it never happens again, I will know that it was real, once.

After that little confession, I closed my eyes so he couldn't see me cry. Crying just pisses me off so much. It's so helpless and girly and *stupid.* He rolled off of me and tucked me up against his front (that hard part was still there but not as much as before). He rested his chin on top of my head and we just lay there for such a long time. It was the best I've ever felt.

After a while he said he had to go home in this hoarse whispery voice, but he wanted to come back tomorrow if it was ok with me. I rolled over and kissed him daringly on his perfect chin and like some sappy, romance, novel heroine, I go, "Nothing would make me happier." Gag. Though it was/is true. He kissed me very, very softly on my lips and then rose out of my bed like Adonis with clothes. I felt sad and small already without him there. He bent over and kissed me again, and then he was gone. I heard him say goodbye to my parents (god, I hope they didn't know what we were doing up here) and then the door shut softly behind him. And that is how it ended, the best day of my life.

Jesse

Eva didn't show up to school for several days, and Jesse was worried. Had she finally cracked? His mom wasn't saying. Eva had been gone for only one day when the bloody writing was written on her locker. Some idiot thought it would be funny to use fake blood to write "witch" across her locker from top to bottom. After school that day, Jesse saw Dave, the school janitor, trying to scrape it off with a plastic putty knife while keeping some of the blue paint on the metal, if possible. He grabbed a spare putty knife from Dave's cleaning cart and helped him scrape the mess off. It had congealed to a hard mass and they took the better part of an hour to finally remove the last bit of it.

"It's such a shame, all these kids picking on that nice girl," Dave said ruefully, as he packed away his cleaning gear. "Bullying is a real problem these days. You see it all over the Internet, kids committing suicide and stuff over this kind of thing. I've told Mr. Herron several times that something's gotta get done about this but he can't seem to catch them. Hey thanks for your help, Jesse, you have a good one." Whistling, he pushed his cart down the hall to stow it back in a closet before heading off to the cafeteria.

Jesse experienced a moment of panic. Surely...Eva wouldn't kill herself because of some dumb kids, would she? He knew she was under a lot of pressure from whatever her illness was. His mom had always been real vague and the teachers would never say. He never saw anything happen because he knew the warning signs too. His mom always told him, "If Eva's eyes roll back in her head, or her hands clench and unclench really fast, you come get me or her mom right away and then you get lost. Ok kiddo?"

and he'd always listened. But with this mental problem she was going through, maybe these rotten kids at school finally set her off.

He whipped out his cell phone and called her house. Her mom answered the phone, and he hung up, not knowing what to say. He'd just have to go by there and see for himself. But surely there would be rumors if she were dead. Wouldn't there? The thought filled his veins with ice.

After a couple of days, Jesse couldn't take it anymore. He called over to her house, staying on the line this time. Eva's mother told him she was sick with some kind of a virus, but he was welcome to visit if he felt like taking his chances. He sighed in relief. He did feel like taking his chances. Definitely.

He told his mom after school the next day that he was headed over there. "No work today, Jess?" she asked.

"No, I'm on later tonight. Don't worry, I'll be back in plenty of time to do my homework."

"I'm not worried. You're a grown boy. You know how to handle your workload. How is Eva? You two haven't been friends in a long time. Why the sudden interest?"

"I just missed her, I guess."

"She's not feeling well, right?"

"How did...oh right, you and her mom are BFF's still. I keep forgetting." He'd never forgotten.

Jesse's mom studied him a moment. Then she said, "Well I'm glad you two kids are talking again. And Jesse...be gentle with Eva, ok? Her life is hard."

Now it was Jesse's turn to stare. "What do you mean? Her parents are great, like you and dad. She's not from a broken home or anything. And if you mean her seizures or whatever, she never said anything about them."

"No, I don't mean the seizures in the way you think. Eva's not like you, Jesse. She's...sensitive...to things. She's different from other girls. Isn't that one of the reasons you like her?" She cocked her head, conveying her meaning without speaking aloud.

Suddenly Jesse felt like a real jerk. What if everything Eva had said to him about that notebook was true? "Thanks Mom," he said in a rush, kissing her cheek and sprinting out to his Jeep.

Jesse drove to the florist and grabbed the biggest bouquet of stargazers he could find. He knew they were Eva's favorite, because it was on her bio for the yearbook. He headed over to her house and parked out by the front lawn, since both her parents were home and their cars took up the driveway. He knocked very politely, and Eva's mom answered with a surprised and pleased smile.

"Jesse! How lovely to see you, and your flowers too!"

"Thanks Mrs. D. Is Eva home?"

"She certainly is. I'll just run up there and make sure she's, you know, up for company." She beamed at him and hustled up the stairs. Jesse made small talk with Eva's dad, who seemed happy to see him. Mr. D grilled Jesse about the football team, and what he thought their chances of a state championship would be this year. Finally, Mrs. D came down the stairs and sent him on up.

He didn't exactly receive a warm welcome. Although she did apologize for what she had said to him last time, he was there. He felt ashamed of how he'd doubted her sanity, so he didn't say anything about her behavior.

Instead, he picked a fight with her about how she acted around him when they were kids, and how confused he'd been about his own feelings toward her, because, obviously, that was her fault. God, he didn't know how to talk to this girl. She made him curse; she made him lose his damn mind. She was maddening! She filled his every waking thought, even when he had supposed she might be crazy. She confused and confounded him. He did the only thing he could think of to stop them from fighting.

He kissed her.

And what a kiss! He wanted it to last forever but he felt her struggling to breathe and finally had to let her up for air. He was kind of guilty about kissing her, knowing she was sick, but he'd never take it back. With that kiss, he'd laid claim to her forever. He was never letting this girl get away from him again.

They cuddled for a while, and he felt powerful, holding her there, and he felt like he belonged. No, more like they belonged to each other. He was apparently a romantic at heart, because he felt like he could lay there with her forever.

She wasn't so bad herself. When he had to leave, very reluctantly, he peeled himself away from her, but not before asking if he could come back tomorrow. Her mercurial moods still made him a little wary. He wasn't fool enough to believe one kiss could tame her. She'd kissed him on the chin and told him nothing would make her happier. His heart swelled so that he thought it might burst out of his chest. Instead he kissed her softly once, twice, and then left. He barely remembered saying goodbye to her parents or driving home. His bed felt pretty cold and lonely that night, but he wrapped himself in the memory of her soft body against his and slept peacefully.

Eva

November 20, 2013

November 21, 2013

Jesse is here right now. He's lying on my bed reading some of my earlier notebooks. We had a good laugh over the one that says "BALLS" over and over. I swear to god if he's not serious about whatever this is that we're doing, I'm going to kill him. God, I'm so freaking stupid. This is going to end BADLY. How can I trust him so quickly after he just left me because he actually liked me of all the stupid reasons? Typical guy thinking. OMG. I've never let anyone read these things in my notebooks. They're like proof of my craziness. Why do I even keep them in the first place? I guess because I want to make sure that I don't forget. It's like these things need me to be a witness or something, and I want to remember everything that's happened to me, everything that's tried to contact me or make itself heard through me. Jesse says that makes a lot of sense and if he had the same ability (he calls it a "gift" because he doesn't know any better) that he'd keep a journal and save the notebooks too.

He came over yesterday like he promised. My parents were both at work; they are both high school teachers; at my school even. It's awful but at least when I was sick they were able to make arrangements for me. Jesse brought me a chocolate croissant because he said it looked like I hadn't eaten in weeks and I couldn't afford to lose any more weight. The jerk. Gosh, I'm really liking his attention though. He got one for himself, too, and he brought us Dutch Brothers. Here in the Pacific Northwest, we have lots of coffee places. Especially in coastal towns like ours, where the wind can feel like it's slicing right through you, coming in off the ocean. We ate and drank our treats in silence cuz I was feeling kind of shy. He didn't kiss me hello or anything so I wondered if he wanted to dial it back and maybe just be friends or something. God, I don't know how to do this. I've never even had a boyfriend for crying out loud. I have no idea how to act. So I just sat there like a lump and not making eye contact.

He finished first and asked if he could read more of my notebook. I said, yeah, thinking he is just hanging out with me because I'm weird, like in an interesting way; like a germ in a petri dish or something. So I muttered, yeah, all intelligently and I said I'd let him read the new one with the parts from when I was sick. I handed it to him and started typing on my laptop, confused and hurt. He was sitting on my bed reading the last time I looked up and then he startled me by saying in my ear, "I'm not here because I think you're interestingly weird, though you are." I jumped in surprise and then swatted him on the arm for scaring me. He laughed and snagged my laptop with one hand and fended me off with the other. The big jerk.

He sat my laptop down gently on the floor and

grabbed me, quick and unexpected. I shrieked a little and giggled like a moron. He laid me down on my bed and hovered above me, supporting himself on one elbow. He got all serious, and he said, "Eva Dunbar, will you be my girlfriend?" like he was proposing or something. I didn't have a clue what to say. Did I want to be his girlfriend? Do I like breathing? Is my heart beating? My stupid mouth utters, "Why? So you can dump me and break my heart again?"

He sighed and let me up. I'm cursing at myself silently, wishing I could crawl under my bed and never come out. He goes, "Eva, what do I have to do to make you trust me?"

And I'm all, "I don't know Jess. I'm sorry. Things just pop out of my mouth."

"I am in love you with Eva. Does that spell it out enough?"

"How do you know you're in love with me? And why after all this time is this just coming out now? You could have come to me and told me all this stuff two, even three, years ago. You just left, without considering how I felt. It's been five years since we really hung out together. You have no idea who I am, anymore."

"Jeez, I was only like twelve years old, Eva. Cut me some slack."

"Well I was only eleven, and you were my best friend, and then you just left! You didn't even talk to me at school. And I saw you walking around with all those perfect blonde hoes and I have never felt like I measured up to them, thanks to you!"

He was pretty quiet for a while. Then he said, "Do you want me to go away?"

I felt my heart race at the idea. I was getting used to having him around again, pretty quickly. In fact I think I've fallen faster than any girl in the history of the world. Did I want him to leave? Not only no, but hell no. But what I said was, "Do you want to go away?"

"No."

"Then don't."

We didn't say anything else for a while. He handed me back my laptop, and then asked if he could read some of my older notebooks since he finished the one I'm on, and I said, "Yeah." I slid the box that I keep them in out from underneath my bed and left them there for him to look at. After a while, he started asking me questions. What did I think the things writing them meant? Did I ever have premonitions, or any other kind of "gifts"?

Finally he put them back in the box and slid it back under my bed. I was at my computer desk typing. He was reading over my shoulder but I didn't mind, especially because I was quick enough to minimize this journal and pretend to be working on makeup assignments. This was a few minutes ago. He said he had to go, but he'd come back after school. Seniors are so lucky. He only has a few classes a day. I said that would be ok, playing it cool, but he didn't let me be cool. He grabbed my hand and pulled me to my feet. He wrapped those strong arms of his around me and pulled me in close, tucking me under his chin and just holding me. I slid my arms around his waist, being unable to help but notice the six-pack under his t-shirt and wishing I had the guts to caress him with my fingertips to feel the contrast of soft skin and hard muscle.

"Eva, you never answered me."

"Mmmmmm," inhaling his scent. He smells so freaking good. Like the ocean and something male, some musky "Jesse Williams" scent.

"Will you be my girlfriend?"

42

I sighed. Whatever. Why not? It was probably going to end badly and hurt like a bastard but I know I'm way too wrapped up in him already. I think about him constantly, even in my dreams.

"Yes."

He pulled back, arms still around me, and searched my eyes in that piercing way of his. He liked what he saw because he pulled out that golden god smile, that megawatt grin, and pressed his lips down on mine. We shared one of those scorching kisses that only happen in movies and books, making my knees actually go weak, pathetically. He kissed my nose then, gently, and gathered his coat, promising again that he'd come back after school. I've been sitting here writing this ever since he left so when it goes bad and he dumps me, I'll have these memories to read again and again.

Jesse

Jesse lay sprawled out on Eva's bed, flipping through the older notebooks she kept in a box hidden under her bed. She explained that sometimes she didn't have a notebook, and she would find random drawings on papers or napkins, anything really that could be written on, and that she threw those away. Still, the ones in the notebooks were frightening. People decapitated, eviscerated, gouged, cut, shot, hung, drowned...the list was endless. Some of them were words with pictures, or just words on the pages. He thought the one that said "BALLS" was funny at first but as he delved further into the collection he began to find it as creepy as the rest.

Eva was sitting at her computer at the desk, kind of ignoring him, which stung his male pride a little. Didn't their kiss mean anything to her? Or did she not feel that way about him? He hated not knowing where he stood with her. But he didn't know how to approach her either. Frustrated, he pulled himself off the bed silently and peered over her shoulder.

"I've never even had a boyfriend, for crying out loud. I have no idea how to act." He read a bit more about her insecure feelings about their budding relationship. Well, well, well...that gave him a surge of hope. He put his lips close to her ear and whispered something flirtatious. They ended up tussling on the bed in the most pleasant manner until he blurted out a question about being his girlfriend. He didn't have much more experience than she did. Yeah, he'd had a couple of girlfriends and had kissed a few times, but for a high school senior he was embarrassingly innocent. He wanted to wait for the right girl, and didn't think it was anyone's business what he knew or didn't know about it. Not that any of the other guys in the locker room knew that. He could talk the talk with the best of them.

Of course, his bumbling attempt at expressing his honest and fervent wish to Eva went over as well as a pet rock can fly. Instead of losing his temper, though, Jesse backed off. He asked if she wanted him to leave, and she threw it back at him. Did he want to leave? That was a no brainer. He stuck around, asking quietly if he could read more notebooks. She wasn't going to get rid of him easily. He was getting use to being in her presence, more quickly than he would have thought. He cursed himself for all those wasted years, for listening to his dumbass brother, and for not being able to find a way to get through her emotional walls. He decided to try a different tack. As soon as he figured out what it was.

And after a while, reading through her notebooks, a thought began to percolate through his brain. What if there was a way to communicate with these things that used Eva's body to break through from wherever they were, in purgatory or wherever? Could he help Eva make them go away?

"Eva, can I ask you a question?"

"Hmm? Sure what's up?" her tone was mild, no longer annoyed and he breathed a sigh of relief.

"What do you think these writings mean? What do you think the intentions of the...things...writing them are?"

She turned to look at him. "What do I think they mean?"

He nodded.

"Well..." she said slowly, as if really thinking about it the first time, or saying it out loud for the first time. "I guess they have to be like spirits or ghosts or something, right? Someone who has something left to say. I think they just want to be heard in some way."

"Do you ever know when it's coming?"

"I don't, but I guess you know about my seizures at school?"

He nodded.

"I can't believe you didn't find out before now, really. Our families have always been so close."

Even when they weren't friends, he thought but didn't say. It was nice of her not to point it out, again.

"Anyway, I guess there are some physical symptoms of a seizure that I have before I have a spirit writing."

He nodded again. "Yeah, I knew about those. We weren't allowed to play together unless I ran to get an adult when I saw it happening, so I never stuck around to see the aftermath. Do you have any other gifts? Like premonition or clairvoyance?"

He could tell from the look on her face she was simultaneously annoyed and impressed.

"You have to stop calling it a gift, Jess. It's really a curse; you have no idea how hard it is. But no, I don't have any of that other stuff."

Jesse nodded a third time and then dropped the subject. He didn't want to antagonize her but he had a plan to find out what these things were, if they were really ghosts or something else, and how to get rid of them, but he needed to do some more research first. He picked up the scattered notebooks and put them back into the box, sliding it under her bed. He stood up and stretched, then read a bit more over her shoulder as she typed. Boring schoolwork was up on the screen, but he wasn't fooled. He knew her journal was still up because it was on the bottom menu bar. He grinned, knowing she couldn't see him, and said he had to get going.

She tried to play like she didn't care that much, but he was hoping she did. He grabbed her hand and pulled her to him, wishing he could run his hands down the soft curve of her spine and press her so close to him they would become inseparable forever. He wondered if she felt the same. He hoped so. But he had some unfinished business of his own before he went home.

"Eva, you never answered me," he reminded her. She tried to play dumb but he wasn't fooled. "Will you be my girlfriend?" he asked again, holding his breath for fear of her saying no to him, again. He braced himself for the pain of rejection, telling himself not to give up, to just give her a little time.

"Yes."

No way. He pulled back, searching her face to see if she was being real. Her amazing sapphire blue eyes sparkled with a blend of emotions. He saw fear, and all the old pain of their past, and even excitement in their depths. He grinned at her, promising silently that he was going to wipe away all the sadness and replace it only with love. He kissed her then, pouring the heat of his promise and the depth of his feelings into the kiss and left before he grabbed her up against him and never let her go.

Eva

November 22, 2013

Getting really tired of seeing this crap in my notebook. Can I buy a vowel please? I don't understand what you want. Me to die? Me to help? I guess Jesse's questions are getting to me, cuz now I want to know what the hell these things want from me.

November 23, 2013

I was super happy when Jesse came back over after school like he said. My parents came home to find us studying in my room like good children, though we had been making out like crazy when we heard their tires crunch on the driveway. Thank god for two-story houses. And they totally trust Jesse because they've known him his whole life. I think my mom can tell stuff is different between us, though, cuz she keeps looking back and forth at us when she thinks I'm not watching. And I swear to god I saw her smirking.

So Dad asked Jesse if he could stay for dinner; Jess texted his mom and told her where he was and what he was doing. She said to tell my mom to call her because there was a change in the PTA meeting and blah, blah, blah. It was a pretty uneventful evening except that JESSE WILLIAMS, MY

BOYFRIEND, WAS AT MY HOUSE FOR DINNER! A month ago, I'd have punched anyone who said such a thing would happen. Go figure.

November 24, 2013
　　　I went over to Jesse's for Thanksgiving, and then he came over to my house for dessert. I told him it's a damn good thing his brother, Aaron, couldn't make it home from college for the holidays, or I might have to deck him for telling Jesse to screw me and get it out of his system when Jess and me were only *twelve and eleven years old*. We have a reckoning coming, Aaron and I.
　　　I have verification that the parental units know that there's something between us because Jesse's mom said how nice it was to see me again and his dad said he was glad we worked it out. They were beaming those William's family megawatt smiles at me, like really friendly sharks. But I love Jesse's parents, I always have. They know I'm not normal but they treat me like I am, and it's really refreshing.
　　　After dessert, we went upstairs to my room. We were super quiet when we kissed so no one would know what we were up to. Then he said he had to go home, and I was all sad and pouty but I understood. It's not like he can live with me now that we're officially together. Get a grip Eva.
　　　But I was kinda worried about school. I was supposed to go back Monday now that whatever I had been sick or possessed by had passed. What was it going to be like? I could only imagine what those assholes had done to my locker while I was gone.
　　　"Can I come by and pick you up in the morning, go out to the beach for a while?" Jess had asked me before he left. I said yes, of course, and he kissed me chastely before leaving, saying he'd see me

tomorrow. Sigh.

November 25, 2013

Killed

November 26, 2013

die in

November 27, 2013

Kill you

kill me

Hey

are wing
die

November 28, 2013

    There has been one of these every day for the
last several days. Starting to get worried. Jesse was

here for the last one. He told me that it was the most frightening thing he'd ever seen in his life, both in movies and in real life. He told me that we were talking, and then my eyes went sort of blank, then filled up with black, like my pupils expanded to cover my entire eyes, and the room got freezing cold. My hands hooked the fingers into claws and I scrabbled at the bed for my notebook and pencil. He told me that one thing he noticed later was the complete lack of sound; he felt like all the sound had been sucked out of the world and filled up my inkjet eyes. I guess I went ahead and scribbled the lovely drawing above this post and then fell back onto the bed, flinging the pencil at the wall my bed sits up against. I threw them so hard that the pencil broke in half.

Then the room got warm, but when I saw Jesse with my own eyes again, all the hairs stood up on his arms and he was pale as, well, a ghost. I was so worried; he looked like he was completely terrified of me. I started crying, naturally; I asked him if he was going to stop being my boyfriend. He shook his head no. He just held me for the longest time.

Jesse was on cloud nine. He had a girlfriend, and it was the girl of his dreams. Eva was smart; wicked smart. But he had to admit her cuteness factor was also a pretty nice perk. Her face was perfect, her skin soft and creamy, her hair dark and lustrous, her eyes luminous, her body smoking hot...he thought about her in terms of textures and shapes, very nice shapes. He thought about her shape a lot.

The time spent with her at her house, or his, was amazing. It was like they'd never left each other as far as their parents were concerned. It was almost eerie, as though they'd seen this coming for years and now he and Eva were playing things out exactly as they'd planned. It sure made things like having dinner at each other's houses and holidays, like Thanksgiving, much easier if both sets of parents were cool with it. Plus they could make out in either one of their bedrooms and get away with it; usually one set of parental units was hanging out at either house or at the school for various functions or meetings. It was totally awesome.

Until the weekend before school, that is. They were hanging out in Eva's room, Jesse laying on her bed stretched out to full length, hoping she would notice his shirt was tucked up a little and his abs were showing. She seemed to have a weakness for his well-toned muscles and he took advantage of it every chance he got. She was sitting at the computer, typing away, and studiously ignoring his display of manliness, but he saw her sneaking peeks now and then. Sometimes he'd read a passage of his book to her. Romeo and Juliet, romantic that he was.

It was great, until suddenly Jesse noticed the

preternatural silence filling the room like helium in a balloon. The pressure in his ears intensified and he looked up at Eva in alarm, to see if she noticed. But what he saw sitting at the computer was no longer the girl he loved.

It was the creepiest thing he'd ever seen in his life, both in movies and in real life. Eva's eyes were completely blacked out, like someone had pricked a hole in the pupils of her eyes and the inky color had bled out into the rest of her eyeball. The room's temperature dropped as fast as the sound left it, and Eva's hands began shaking, her fingers curled into claws, seeking, seeking, seeking something...she lurched for the bed and Jesse launched himself out of her way. Her demon hands scrabbled at the notebook and pencil she kept at the headboard and she began scribbling furiously in it, rocking back and forth. She made absolutely no sound and she didn't appear to see anything.

As soon as she was finished scribbling, or whatever had finished using her body was done, she threw the notebook and pencil against the wall her bed rested against with unexpected violence. Jesse jumped in fear, then stood there watching. Eva fell back against the bed, her back arched and only her head and heels touching the mattress. Jesse watched, terrified for her but afraid to touch her, afraid whatever it was would come back, wondering if he should go for an adult. As soon as he thought it, though, the room's temperature began to thaw and sound began to seep back into the world, slow and faint at first but soon back to normal.

Well, everything was back to normal except Jesse.

Eva lay still on the bed, but after a moment, her eyelids fluttered open and she looked at Jesse with her own, normal, beautiful eyes.

Jesse felt as though he may never sleep again. What had just happened to his girl was about the worst thing he'd ever imagined. He didn't know how he could look at her again, how he could be around her when she was taken over by whatever the hell it was, spirits, or ghosts, or fuck even demons. He didn't know. The hair on his neck and arms stood out in reaction to the adrenaline and fear coursing through his body, even though the apparent danger was gone. He watched Eva recognize his fear and saw her eyes fill with tears. She was obviously afraid of the very things he'd been thinking a moment before.

"Are you going to break up with me?" her voice quavered.

He shook his head no. How could he leave her now?

And when she started crying, without the usual rage that accompanied her tears, Jesse's paralyzing horror subsided and he gathered the girl he loved in his arms and just held her, for the longest time.

Eva

December 2, 2013

Today was my first day back at school since right before Halloween. Most of my teachers were really nice except, Clausen, that jerk. He docked points from my MacBeth assignment since I wasn't in class to participate in the discussions, though Jesse and I had finally gotten around to doing some homework and my questions were spot on. Even McGhee was nicer to me than that a-hole.

Nothing can bring me down right now, though. I haven't had any writings in my notebook in a few days, after that blitz the week before school. And the best part is that Jess is with me in public at school too. Like he picks me up and drives me in his awesome Jeep Willys that's all retro, and amazing looking, holds my hand in the hallway, sits by me in chemistry. It's literally all I can freaking do not to stick my tongue out at that she-dog, Natasha, every single time. And we have lunch together at his table. His friends, who I always thought of as unevolved gorillas, are all really nice to me and make me feel ashamed of the mean things I thought about them. Ok a little ashamed. They're still high school boys, therefore unevolved gorillas.

Jess read that over my shoulder and started tickling me. We ended up on my bed kissing of course.

December 12, 2013

Today at school was the best day ever. That evil, bitch, Natasha, was making snide comments about Jesse slumming it with me in chemistry today, and he said, "No that was when I was hanging out with you. I've always loved Eva." HE SAID LOVED ME IN PUBLIC!!! *Like. A. Boss.* In front of that whore too!

I was floating on cloud nine and then, at lunch, a couple of Natasha's friends came to the table Jess and me were eating at and sat down. I know they just came to sit with their boyfriends, who are friends with Jesse, but they were really nice. I guess they finally made their choice who to hang out with; teenage hormones win every time. I mean, I knew all of them but never hung out with them; after all, this is Brookings. Everyone knows everyone.

They were talking about the Winter Formal and the guys were talking to Jess about getting a limo, and I swear to god, Beth Nichols turns to me and started talking to me about dresses. She's never even looked at me before. I wanted to be all high and mighty, but Jess winked at me over her head and resumed his conversation, so I mentally shrugged and started talking fashion. Like I know anything about it, me, the hoodie queen.

Beth's father owns a boutique in Eugene and he said Beth and a friend could have their pick of dresses. And she asked me to go with her next weekend! I never thought I'd be excited to go shopping for dresses with Beth Nichols, but I actually am. And the best part was the look on that hag, Natasha's face when she saw all of her friends sitting with Jess and me. She huffed and flung her blond locks behind her shoulder like we cared. I saw out of the corner of my eye where she went over and sat with the emo/goth kids, flirting outrageously with Justin Perkins, the boy with the black, spiky Mohawk and multiple face piercings. As if that was going to make Jesse jealous or something. HA!

December 16, 2013

I feel almost normal. I haven't had any troubles lately, and Jesse and I are inseparable. I go with him a lot to the beach while he takes pictures and it's so nice to feel like I belong to someone, especially someone as wonderful as Jesse. I finally told him I loved him, too, the other day when we were at the beach. He kissed me and held me close for a while. Then, he asked if I was going to go dress shopping with Beth and I said I guess so.

He said, "Why, do you have a date?" all innocently.

I felt really stupid right about then. I mean, he hadn't even asked me, I just assumed…and then he started laughing, so I had to tackle him in the sand. He kissed me and I growled, "Not so fast, buddy," and bit him less than gently on the lip. Being about a foot taller and way stronger, naturally he was easily able to flip me on my back and hold me down to kiss me at his leisure. Finally, he stopped for a moment to let me get my breath.

"Oh, beautiful and desirable, Evalyn Dunbar, will you please do me the eternal honor of accompanying me to the Brookings High School Winter Formal?"

"I'll think about it!"

"Maybe a good tickling will change your attitude!"

"Oh god, Jess, please no! I'll go, I'll go!"

He tickled the crap out of me anyway, smugly sure that I was absolutely going to the dance with him; that jerk. Of course, I'm gonna.

Having Eva back at school, and openly his girl in public where everyone could see was one of the most satisfying and happiest experiences of Jesse's life so far. After he had seen Eva have one of her spirit-writing episodes, he made the conscious decision to do whatever it took to help her get rid of it. He had felt that it was a gift, before he saw it for himself. Now he knew better. If they couldn't make it stop, they'd need to figure out a way to deal with it. He resolved to be there for the rest of her episodes of spirit writing, so that it wouldn't freak him out anymore and so he could be supportive. He was ashamed of his cowardice when he'd seen it the first time and hoped she never found out. It wasn't that he'd doubted he loved her. He didn't. It was just so freaky, like a horror movie. He tried to cut himself some slack and blame it on shock, but his guilt made him lavish her with attention and gifts.

She seemed to really enjoy hanging on his arm in the hallways and he swore he saw her stick her tongue out at Natasha one day when he dropped her off at her Economics class. He loved picking her up in the mornings and stopping for coffee, then driving to school with her by his side. He always made sure to open her doors for her and drop kisses on her forehead when teachers were looking, and kisses of the more scorching hot kind when they weren't. He was glad his friends were nice to her too. His buddy, Eric, had been his best friend since the beginning of high school, and he and his girlfriend, Beth, were the most welcoming of Eva, out of all of Jesse's friends.

"Dude, I'm just glad to see you with a girl. I thought you were going into a monastery or some shit," was Eric's only comment about Jesse's new love life.

Natasha was a little bit bitchier about it. One day in chemistry she said, "I guess Jesse just needed to be the prettiest one in the relationship."

Jesse was pissed. He knew her life was hard, but talking shit about his girl was going too far. He'd gone through too much self-doubt and guilt, lost too much time, and loved Eva far too much to let some skank say mean shit about her that wasn't true. He loudly proclaimed that he'd loved Eva for years and he'd only hung out with Natasha, because she made him look better by comparison. That pretty much broke things with Natasha; she stopped speaking to him after that, but honestly, he didn't even notice she was gone. His eyes were filled with the sight of Eva.

Lunch was pretty cool, because all his friends and their girls were super-awesome to Eva. He was a little surprised when Beth started singling Eva out for girl time. She had been one of Natasha's friends but apparently didn't like her bitchiness either. She'd been bad-mouthing both Eva and him to Beth and Eric, and they both told her to take a hike. Jesse was glad when Beth invited Eva to go dress shopping. He knew Eva was more of a tomboy. He grinned at Eric, knowing Beth would have a hard time divorcing Eva from her hoodie sweatshirts and jeans. Then he saw Natasha hanging out at the emo kids' table with that Justin Perkins kid and frowned. The way Natasha made friends with guys was to sleep with them. He knew, because she'd tried it with him and he'd turned her down. Even though she wasn't his friend anymore, he didn't think she should be hanging out with that kid. She had enough problems as it was. He had heard some things about him at Eric's house, from Eric's dad, who was a cop. He and Eric shared another look, and Eric nodded slightly. He'd tell his old man about Natasha's new best friend. It was part of a case of child abuse the old man was trying to put together against Natasha's family and this would be another nail in the coffin for her fucked up parents.

Jesse was getting used to having Eva in his life pretty fast. Her episode was never far from his mind, but she didn't have any for such a long time he sort of hoped they were gone for good. He took her to the beach almost every day after school, watching her play in the waves if it was nice or walk along next to them, barefoot in the sand, if it was not.

His passion was photography; he took endless photos of her next to the sparkling water. One particularly nice day, he walked next to her, holding her hand, his camera dangling from the other hand.

She stopped and put her small hand on his chest, looking up into his face with solemnity. "I love you, Jesse," she said with such serious intent he couldn't help but smile, both at her expression and her words. He kissed her and drew her close, listening to her heart beating against him.

Finally, they broke apart and continued their walk. They started talking about the Winter Formal, and Jesse was interested in the color dress she might pick so he could get a matching corsage. He teased her a little, then asked her formally to the dance with him. She teased him back, and they ended up wrestling and making out in the sand.

Eva

December 20, 2013

Since I decided to give Jesse another chance in my life, everything has gotten better and better. The episodes of spirit writing have decreased, which is awesome by me. And our parents have started hanging out again, since their kids are together all the time at one house or the other. It's nice to see the parental units having fun, playing board games and drinking wine like they used to when we were little kids.

I went shopping with Beth! I found the most beautiful dress at her dad's shop. She said it makes my black hair and blue eyes "dazzle" the eye. LOL! She, being of blond and blue-eyed stock, was naturally a knockout, but it was nice of her to say those things. Her dress is pink and she got pink satin pumps a shade darker to go with her dress. It's a sort of Grecian style, one shoulder bare and the other covered, and fits her curves really well. If she weren't so nice to me, I'd be super-jealous. Ok, I'm super-jealous anyway. But she's not as much of a bimbo as that bitch, Natasha. I wonder why she ever hung out with her? Who knows, at least she isn't trying to steal Jesse; Beth dates Eric Carlson, one of the football players who hangs out with Jesse, whose dad is a deputy in town and whose mom died, when we were little kids, of breast cancer. Poor Eric. Him and Beth are really good together, though, he treats her really well and she seems crazy about him.

MY dress is the best one, I think. It's a pale shimmery blue number, off the shoulder, with a flaring skirt and tight bodice that has stays in it. That makes me look like I have boobs and gives the illusion of a butt. I got the same shade of blue on my little pumps, and some new makeup and hair accessories. Beth promised she would do my hair and makeup for the dance too. It's on Sunday, so I'll be sure to write down every moment when I get back!

December 22, 2013

Tonight was magical. I know that's a cliché but it's so fitting. I'm completely exhausted and my feet hurt, but I couldn't be happier. Beth came over super early and did my hair and makeup, and then did hers too. She left right before it was time for Eric to come by with the limo so he could pick her up in it. Jesse showed up at eight, and he looked so freaking handsome in his black tux, freshly shaved and his hair all disarrayed charmingly in that way I love. It made my heart literally hurt in my chest to see how beautiful he was.

I came downstairs carefully, not that I'm super clumsy, but I could just see falling all the way downstairs and landing in a crumpled heap at Jesse's feet. I had no plans to end up in the hospital tonight, like that stupid girl in the Twilight books. Anyway, the look on his face when he saw me made me feel indescribable, like I was valuable to him, that I mattered, and normal, like a normal girl with a normal handsome boyfriend.

Usually I wonder how I deserved him but not tonight. His expression told me I deserved him and he was happy to deserve me. My parents naturally interfered with their exclamations and photos and insisting on having us pose a million times! Eric and Beth showed up with the limo, and got to have their picture taken too. We had fun making googly faces when the parents weren't looking.

Finally we got to leave. The limo driver was really patient, LOL. We picked up two other couples that I know of, but don't know well, you know? Dayna Bishop and her boyfriend Michael Sooner, and Jason North and his girlfriend from out of town, Jessica something. They seemed nice; Michael and Jason, of course, are two of Jesse's other football friends. I like Eric and Beth better, but it was cheaper to have more people in the limo. I was kinda sad to see it drive off after it dropped us off, but Jesse and the guys had all parked their cars at school so we could go our separate ways. I think some of them wanted to be alone later, if you know what I mean.

The gym looked really awesome; the decorating committee did a great job! It was a Winter Under the Sea theme, which is so wrong considering we live by the ocean and we're not eighty, but it worked, somehow. The magic of Winter Formal, I guess. There were icicles and frozen waves, and fish and mermaids in blocks of ice, and a giant freaking disco ball, I kid you not. Jesse and I danced all night, literally, only stopping to use the restroom and grab refreshments. Sometimes, during a slow song, we just clung to each other and barely swayed from side to side. People danced over to us and talked to us, like Beth and Eric, which was cool. They stayed by us most of the night. One time, we danced by them and Beth said, "You guys look like the sun and the moon, glowing with different lights but complementing each other really well." It was one of the nicest things I've ever heard.

We all got a good laugh at Natasha showing up with that strange looking Jeremy kid. Not that I have anything against him, if he wants to punch holes in his face that's really not my business. And I was once labeled a goth/emo kid, so I wasn't about to cast stones at him, though that's all changed for me once Jesse and I started dating.

His date, however, looked like she had shopped at Whores R Us. Natasha was wearing a black leather sheath dress, to a dance! Everything was black, of course, and she had on these hooker boots that went up her very short dress to god knows where. But she made it a point to bend over now and then and flash the room; clearly she forgot to put on her leather thong. Jesse and Eric both made sounds of disgust which was nice of them considering they are, after all, teenage boys getting a free peek at girl parts. That was the only bad part of the night though.

Jesse brought me home by one after we had coffee with Eric and Beth at Denny's, and kissed me sweetly at the door. It was the perfect evening.

Jesse

When he saw her coming down those stairs, Jesse Williams knew that he would do anything, anything at all, to make Eva Dunbar his forever. Yes, they were young. Yes, they had a long way to go. But Jesse believed in true love and soulmates and the bolt of longing, love, and even pain in his chest was a tangible ache. He put his hand to his heart and vowed to remember that moment for as long as he lived. His eyes sparkled with emotion as he watched her every move.

The night of the Winter Formal was a blast. When Jesse picked Eva up for the dance, the sight of her coming down her stairs in that blue, shimmery, off-the-shoulder dress literally took his breath away. He finally knew how that felt, having read it in books but never experiencing it for himself. She was the most beautiful girl in the world. And she was all his.

Apparently Natasha had shown up at the dance all decked out in leather and flashing the place. Eric said he saw her but averted his eyes so he didn't piss Beth off. Jesse never even saw her. He had eyes only for Eva.

It was tempting—God, so tempting—to consummate their relationship on the night of the formal dance. But Jesse knew that Eva was the one. He planned to spend the rest of his life making love to her and wanted to do it right, the first time, every time. So he kissed her chastely on her porch steps and watched as she went inside, making his lonely way home but cherishing every moment of the evening, savoring it like chocolate, long into the night.

Eva

December 26, 2013

Christmas was amazing! Jesse bought me a diamond necklace in the shape of a heart! I'm never taking it off. I got him a new stereo for his Jeep, complete with installation and new speakers and woofers and thingies that go with stereos. I dunno, but it was my dad's idea so I ran with it.

Dad and Mom both helped me make the appointment and Dad drove me down there to pay for it with my summer pet-sitting money. I can't drive yet because my parents were worried that I'd have an "episode" while driving, so I don't have a 'real' job like Jesse's gig fishing during the summer. It's ridiculous. A girl needs to be able to lavish her guy with gifts!

December 28, 2013

Horrible day. Found this in my notebook:

And I'm pretty sure that slut, whore, Natasha has been putting those nasty notes in my locker. I'm so sick of her shit!

December 29, 2013

When Jesse got here today with my coffee, I was still in bed. My parents were out doing parent stuff. I have no idea where they went. I was sleeping when they left. He didn't get an answer so he just used the hide a key and let himself in. I guess I looked pretty bad because he sat the coffee on the desk and came to the bed and grabbed me up, blankets and all. He hugged me pretty tight and stroked my hair down my back, which I liked. I relaxed a little bit and sank into him. He makes everything better.

"What's wrong, baby?"

"I'm just bummed. I was starting to feel like a real girl." I lifted my head and gave him a small smile. He kissed the corner of my mouth absently and tucked me back against him, holding my head.

"What do you mean? Is there another…thing in your notebook?"

"Yeah. There hasn't been one in a while. I guess I was just hoping it was gone, you know?"

"I know. Don't be scared. I'm here for you, you know that, don't you?"

I sighed with exasperation. "I'm not scared of it, Jess, I just hate it! I just want to be like everyone else, like you, or Beth, or even that hateful bitch, Natasha, with her perfect teeth and her perfect boobs and her perfect life."

"Natasha is not perfect, Eva. And her life is pretty far from perfect."

"Oh, and how do you know that?" I could feel my eyes narrowing and voice getting snippier but I couldn't stop myself.

"We *were* kind of friends; at least, we hung out with the same people, but they picked you over her. And so did I. There was really no contest, don't you see? Doesn't that make you feel a bit sorry for her?

Everyone gets tired of Natasha after a while."

I sighed again. I was not going to fight with the guy I love about some horrible girl we go to school with. Looming on the horizon was an even bigger fight that I wasn't looking forward to. In less than a year, Jesse was going to graduate. I still had a year of high school. I was pretty sure I was going to lose him and never recover from it. I pushed off from his chest and reached for my coffee on the computer desk, opening the lid to my laptop so it could fire up, its dinosaur-like insides.

"Is that your newest notebook on the bed?"

"Yep. You wanna look at it? It's the same one again. I'm ready for a different channel."

"You shouldn't joke about it, Eva. It worries me; why doesn't it scare you?"

"Because I've dealt with it my whole life, Jess. Since I was one and could hold a crayon. I have had a long time to get used to it."

He didn't say anything else but picked up my notebook, which I had doodled a picture of the Grim Reaper on the front of. He made no comment but arched a perfect golden eyebrow at me. I giggled and handed him his coffee. I turned to my laptop and started typing; I had a creative writing paper due in Clausen's class when we got back from Christmas break and I wanted to surprise the old, turkey buzzard by handing mine in first. It's a glorious tale of true love, and a golden knight in shiny armor, and a dark witch who casts a love spell on him, only to have the spell be reversed and backfire on her. The only stipulation was that we had to use an original piece of art to base our story on. I was firing up the Internet to do a search for famous works of art as inspiration, when I heard Jesse say a very bad word very loudly.

"What?"

"Eva, this is freaking creepy. The same thing has been using you to write for months. Have you ever just asked any of these things what they want?"

"I told you, honey, I can't do that," I said, really frustrated. He's asked me this already. I've tried to explain that when this happens, I'm not here. Like my body is here, and obviously my hands are here, but I'm not in control. I have no memory of these things happening, let alone any presence of mind to like be asking questions.

"What if…" he started, slow, like he was working it out in his head or worried what I'd say.

"Go on…"

"What if I was here for one, and I asked questions, just to see what would happen? Maybe it will answer me if I ask it what it wants."

"The last time you saw me have one, you were scared of me. I don't think I could stand it if you were afraid of me or didn't love me anymore, Jess."

"I was scared Eva, but not of you, *for* you."

This led to holding, hugging, and kissing, a little light petting maybe. Oh, god, I can feel myself blushing writing this. But it's true; things are starting to heat up between us.

Finally, I pushed him off me and sat up. His idea has merit. I told him we could try it if he's here for another one. He asked if we can "bring it on" and it took me a sec to get my head out of the gutter and figure out what he meant. Go Eva! A dirty mind is a terrible thing to waste, they say.

"No, I've never found a way to make one happen. But maybe you should have a list of questions to ask if and when it happens when you're here."

He agreed and told me I was a genius. HA! I love him. He's super, and mine, mine, mine. He typed up a list on my laptop and says I'm not supposed to see it in case that messes up our experiment. So I'm not looking at the Word doc on my desktop labeled, "Questions from Beyond," for science.

Jesse

He'd found the necklace in a jewelry shop downtown. The shopkeeper, a nice old lady with silver hair and a gentle smile, had told him that the piece belonged to a young woman whose husband had gone away to the war long ago and never returned. He felt sad for that lady who had lost her necklace and her husband, and knew that Eva would be as taken in by the story as he was.

He was so surprised by Eva's gift he didn't know what to say at first. He knew she loved cruising the twisty Redwood Highway and the 101 with him, the Jeep hugging the curves in the road and the radio blasting. They had similar taste in music and never argued about the song choice, which was a nice surprise when he'd discovered it. The new sound system she'd had installed in his Jeep meant more than her wish to please him. To Jesse, it showed that she planned to stick around for a while and listen to the music they loved together. And that was the best part of the present in his opinion.

He'd enjoyed giving her the necklace and explaining the story behind it as he slipped it on, clasping the small chain around her slender neck while she held her fabulous dark hair out of the way. He planted a kiss on her exposed skin, watching with pleasure as she got goosebumps and shivered slightly.

He felt pretty lousy when, a few days after Christmas, he showed up at her house and found her in bed, lethargic and depressed. There had been another episode, and he missed it. Not only that but he'd almost forgotten about her spirit writing with the excitement of the Winter Formal and holidays. She hadn't had one for a while and he was kinda hoping they were gone, but in the back of his mind he knew better.

She claimed she wasn't afraid, but he knew she was. Hell, he was afraid but he was more determined than ever to get to the bottom of it and try to make it stop. He flipped through the new notebook while Eva slid over to the computer so he could stretch out on the bed, but with every page he flipped through, Jesse's frustration grew until he couldn't contain it any more.

"FUCK!"

Eva turned. "What?"

Jesse knew he'd already covered this with her but he couldn't help it. He wanted her to ask them what they wanted. Now was as good a time as any to tell her his idea about him asking the next spirit that used her body to communicate what the hell it wanted. She didn't respond as badly as he'd thought she would and eventually, after some serious making out, she gave him the green light to make a list of questions to ask it. Jesse was determined to get some answers and protect the girl he loved.

Eva

December 31, 2013

I'm going to Jesse's tonight to celebrate New Year's; my parents are going, too, to hang out with the Williams'. Jess and I were going to go hang out with Eric and Beth at her house for a New Year's Eve party. Jesse called it a New Year's Eva party. He's such a loveable dork. We decided against the party, cuz our parents would let us have champagne as long as we're at home and not driving. That sounded pretty good to us so we're gonna watch a movie upstairs and give the old fogey's the downstairs to party their butts off. Haha. I bet we had more fun than they did, making out all night. Wink wink.

* * * *

Oh, god, I forgot to write this down. So humiliating. My mom asked me if Jesse and me were using protection. That's how she worded it: using protection. UGH! Nothing like the "sex talk" to make you feel awkward and creeped out by your parents. I'm glad it was my mom and not my dad though. I can't imagine that conversation. I told my mom, not that it's her business, that Jess and me aren't doing "it" yet.

She was all cool and stuff and she said, "Well Eva, I was young once, too, as evidenced by your existence, and while you are a delight and a joy, I want you to experience more out of life before becoming a mother. So I'll tell you what: I'll prepay for a doctor's visit and you just go in whenever you feel like you need to and that will be all I have to say about the matter, okay?"

Now that I think about it, my mom is super cool, kind of a hippie in a way, but really a smart lady. I'm not ready but it's nice to know she's got my back.

January 1, 2014
It happened last night. I didn't have my laptop, it was in my room, so Jesse improvised. He remembered most of the pretyped questions. He's a genius like that, remembers everything. It's kind of exciting because this is the first time I've ever had anything like this happen, although it really freaked Jesse out. When I came back to myself, he was shaking and holding me really tight; I could hardly breathe. I'm like, "Ease up baby, I'm ok."

"Oh my god Eva, that was amazing and horrible at the same time!"

"Really? What happened?"

"I'll show you in a minute, just let me sit here a sec. I'm kinda spooked."

So we sat there and I held him for a change until he felt better. Then he said he'd go through it with me and I said well let's do it on my laptop, so we walked to my house. It was dark, and we could hear the sounds of the waves crashing on shore. Jesse held my hand really tightly and I didn't complain. By then I was pretty spooked, too.

Here is what happened while I was away from my body. I put in Jesse's questions and then scanned in the answers.

Who are you?

Alex

Why are you here?

Dead

What do you want?

Evangeli

How did you die?

drowned

Where are you now?

deadbutwaterbutthis

How can Eva help you?

stop

That's as far as we got before the really frightening thing happened, Jesse said. He told me that my eyes were rolled up in my head so only white parts showed and my eyelids flickered really quickly the whole time. Then I threw down the pen after I wrote "stop" and flung my notebook behind me on the bed. I kinda hunched over and just sat there motionless for a really long time. He got worried so he reached over and touched my shoulder, and I flung myself on him really fast, catlike, and he fell back on the bed with me riding on top of him and my eyes still all fluttery and white and I go, "Jeeeesssssseeee Willlliaaaaammmmms" in a whispery, not-Eva voice and fell on him.

He said it was super freaking cold in his room and my body was frozen, rigid, against him, and the light bulb in his room suddenly just went out. He told me later that he was honestly considering pushing me off him and getting help. I can't blame him. That's never happened before, but I've almost always been alone when I spirit write, except for when my parents have seen and they never said anything about something like this happening. But I think maybe it's time I had a talk with them.

Luckily, the light from his TV was enough for him to see so he wasn't completely in the dark with his possessed girlfriend. God, am I doing the right thing by involving Jesse in this? What if he gets hurt somehow? I'll never forgive myself.

Jesse said he could tell immediately that it was over as soon as the light bulb went out because everything warmed up and I sagged against him, and my body started to warm up too. He was holding me super tight, like I said, when I came back.

We sat quietly on my bed for a while after he told me all this and we had scanned the notebook pages into my journal. I finally had to break the silence.

"Are you going to break up with me?"

"God no, Eva. I'm just so worried for you. This thing didn't really tell us much."

I was never happier to hear him say no to me.

"Sure it did, babe. We have a name. I think it's been trying to tell me its name for a while. There's sometimes that funny little mark in the lower corner; now that I think about it, I guess that's an "A", right?"

"I think you're right, now that you say it. As weird and terrifying as that was, I'm kind of glad it happened. Now maybe we can get to the bottom of this and make it go away."

That made me feel sad. Didn't he understand that it was never going to go away? This is part of who I am.

I felt his strong fingers under my chin as he lifted my face to his. "I meant this particular ghostie, sweetheart. I love and accept you in all your forms, even the creepy scary ones."

"Gee thanks! What a resounding endorsement of love from the man I plan to marry!"

Oh. Hell. Why, Eva, why, why, why? What's worse is, he said nothing. A smile curved his perfect lips and that was all. I guess I'm kind of glad he let it drop. After all, we're just kids. It's a fantasy I have, really, that he'll wait for me, we'll go to college together, and live happily ever after, only in fairy tales, Eva, not nightmares.

New Year's Eve was amazing. They had planned to go to Eric and Beth's party, but their parents offered them not only some champagne but alone time too. Jesse knew that both sets of parents worried about what they might be doing but trusted them to behave. It was getting more and more difficult to live up to that trust as the days went by, and New Year's Eve was no exception. The taste of champagne on Eva's lips fueled the fire and he'd finally had to stop them with a movie and some pillows between them. Eva pouted at him in the most adorable manner but he was not dissuaded. If he touched her again, he would no longer be responsible for his actions so he stayed on his side of the pillows.

The next day it happened and he was ready, or so he thought. They were at his house watching TV in his room, so the questions they'd typed on the laptop were at her house, but he remembered most of them. Not that it was easy to question her when she was possessed by something else. It freaked him out to see her hand, her delicate hand that he held tenderly when they walked together, jerking around on the paper and scratching out shapes and words in an unfamiliar writing.

As he asked the questions, and the thing using Eva's body answered, he could feel the sweat breaking out on his body. As before, all the sound in the world bled from existence and the polar temperature of the room froze the sweat pouring from him before he could wipe it away.

As soon as the last question was finished, Eva's eyes rolled back into her head and the whites gleamed in her face, almost glowing in the dim light of his room. She flung the paper and pen away like before, but this time she launched herself at him and whispered, "Jeeeesssseeee Wiiiiilllliaaaaammmmsss." Her fingers gripped his shirt tightly and she pulled him closer and closer, the whites of her eyes jiggling in her head. The light bulb in his room burst, and he almost pushed her off of him to run and get someone but then it was over.

Once the thing was gone, Jesse gathered Eva in his arms and rocked her back and forth until she came back to him.

"Ease up baby, I'm ok."

Jesse was glad he'd handled himself better than the last time, but he was still pretty freaked. Finally, he was able to tell her what had happened and they looked over the spirit writing session's answers together. She was worried, as usual, that he was going to break up with her but he dismissed that. There was no way he was leaving.

"It says its name is 'Alex'," Eva pointed out.

"I'm glad this happened. Now we can make it go away!"

She looked downcast at that. He knew why, and he did his best to reassure her, his message serious but delivered with some teasing. Then she said, "What a resounding endorsement of love from the man I plan to marry!"

Marry! She said marry. He heard it. He felt his chest swell with pride and love. This girl made him feel like he was invincible, and he was more confident than ever that they were going to get to the bottom of this spirit-writing thing and conquer it together. He was glad she had said that she wanted to marry him, because he had no idea how to bring up the subject himself. He knew he wanted to marry her, when they were both done with school and college, of course.

He decided to go ring shopping soon. Maybe his mom could help him out. They were too young now, but he wanted to claim her as his own as soon as possible.

Eva

January 3, 2014

Jesse hasn't said anything else about my fanciful schoolgirl stupidity, which is good. We have moved past that and are trying to decode the answers to those questions. Who is Alex? Where is he from? How did he drown? Is his body still in the water somewhere? Is that what "dead in the water" means? We typed these questions up and sent a copy to Jesse's house. He's printed them and they are here on my computer as well. We're ready for Alex to come back whenever he's ready to talk to us again.

January 7, 2014

I have had enough of this waiting around crap; still nothing from our resident ghostie. Jess thinks I need to talk to my parents. I said, "Negatory Batman" and he just rolled his eyes at me and kissed me. I get so distracted by those kisses! Next thing I know, I have agreed to talk to the 'rents about my freaky past. And my pushy boyfriend who was READING OVER MY SHOULDER was going to COME WITH ME instead of making me do it by myself!

He really liked the comment about kissing though. So we did that for a while until it got too intense. I like that when I sit up and smack him on the leg or arm like a real smooth person would do. He just grinned and tried to mess up my hair. The big jerk. I really think he's the guy for me. I always have, I guess. I'm in horrible danger of losing my morbid, mopey, goth-y reputation and becoming all fan girl over Jesse Freaking Amazing Greek God Williams. Even bitchy McGhee the PE Geek, and Mr. Clausen the English Doom Guy can't bring me down. Though they are trying really hard. McGhee makes us run laps until our legs feel like jello because it's too cold to "play outside" she said. We're freaking teenagers. We don't play outside anyway. And Clausen was actually being really cool. He let us pick our own books to do reports on to "get back in the swing of things" after the Christmas holiday. He must have noticed things were looking up for me cuz Jesse dropped me off at Yearbook today with a smooch, and Clausen said, "Nice catch, Dunbar." I was pretty shocked but you know that Clausen guy is ok.

January 8, 2014

We talked to my parents today. Let me just say right here for the record that if Jessie decides never to speak to me again I will completely understand. I don't want to speak to me ever again either. They told us about some of the other creepy things that have happened since I was a baby. Like one time, there was a spirit or whatever they are that kept writing on the frost on my window from the OUTSIDE. How the eff did it do that? That wasn't the same as spirit writing because I wasn't doing that. That's never happened where I can remember, unless it did happen and then melted before I was "awake" or able to see it.

The parental units were really shaken up talking about the whole thing, but I think they were glad to finally get it aired out. Though I feel way worse about myself, unfortunately. They had some great ideas, though. They suggested asking more questions and were glad Jesse's there for me. Dad got all teary-eyed thinking about the perfect match his little girl has made. Eva is exasperated. Yes I just referred to myself in the third person. Maybe that would help me to feel as though all this stuff is happening to someone else, some other poor messed up girl.

January 9, 2014
It happened again today. This time we were ready. Here is the "transcript" of what Jesse and the spirit using me to write talked about.
What is your last name?

How did you die?

How old were you when you died?

Did you live here in Brookings or somewhere else?

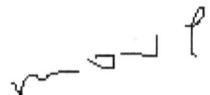

What do you want?

How can Eva help you?

How can Jesse help you?

Where are you now?

Jesse handled this time a lot better than last time. When I came back to myself he was holding me and rocking a little bit, but he wasn't all freaked out and pale. We spent some time talking about the answers to our questions. We couldn't figure out what the message was to how Jesse can help and where he was from. It looks like it says "move" but that doesn't really answer the question. I guess, unless he moved to somewhere, or from somewhere? And what does it mean "dead in the water"? Is his body somewhere in water? Maybe he wants us to find his body. We couldn't come up with too many answers, but we both agree that the name, Alex Carmichael, rings a bell dimly in the back of our minds.

I begged Jesse to let it go; usually these things go away, but he insists that if we figure out what Alex Carmichael wants us to do that he'll go away faster. I'm not pushing too hard, really, since I'm getting to spend so much time with him. I just wish our time together wasn't focused so much on my weirdness.

Jesse

Jesse knew that Eva had been dealing with everything that happened to her for a long time and had covered it pretty well. But he had no idea how much she kept inside until he'd seen it a couple of times for himself. He admired her more, now that he knew.

Talking to her parents was enlightening for Jesse. He couldn't imagine if his kid had something like this following her around, how he would act. He was grateful to them in a way, for providing her with as normal a life as they could and not making a big deal out of it. They seemed pretty happy he was around which made him feel pretty good, too.

He was more prepared the third time it happened.

He knew Alex Carmichael. When the thing using Eva's body wrote that, every blood cell in Jesse's body froze solid. He told Eva that he would do some research but he remembered exactly who Alex Carmichael was. When Eva came back to herself, they talked about it for a while but Jesse was preoccupied. He knew exactly where to go to get the information he needed, too.

Eva

January 12, 2014

It was Jesse that remembered Alex Carmichael; I guess I was too wrapped up in losing his friendship at the time to remember what had happened. Jesse found a newspaper clipping at the library from when we were in grade school about Alex's drowning. His body was found at Haystack Rock, drowned and bloated. Here's a copy of the microfilm (Jesse took a picture with his cell phone):

Brookings, ORE.   75 Cents | 3 Sections, 32 Pages   December 14, 2007

Homerun:
Angels defeat the Pelicans at home. See page B-5 for highlights.

THE CURRIER

SPECIAL REPORT
Local Boy Found Washed Ashore
By Stephanie Young (Staff Writer)

December 14, 2007: This idyllic stretch of beach is the location where an early morning jogger found the body of young Alex Carmichael. (Photos courtesy of Stephen Victor, staff photographer)

The body of young Alex Carmichael washed ashore early this morning along an idyllic stretch of Brookings Harbor Beach, along Haystack Rock side. Police say the young boy was climbing along Haystack Ridge (shown below) when he fell into the water, hitting his head on the way down and landing in the water, unconscious. The boy is suspected to have drowned as a result of his injuries. An autopsy is scheduled for next Tuesday; in the meantime, his family, friends, and classmates mourn his loss.

Memorial Services are pending the conclusion of the autopsy for young Alex Carmichael. The family is asking for donations to the World Wildlife Foundation in Alex's name, in lieu of flowers. Contact Bea Cicco at Memorial Garden for more information.

Family Unconvinced
AP-Dec. 14, 2007 5:21 PM

The family of the dead boy insist that their son would never have gone to the beach alone. "Alex was a great kid, and he knew the rules," his father, Aaron Carmichael told reporters today. "He was also a very strong swimmer. If he fell in the water, there's no way he would have drowned. He grew up here. He knew how to handle himself."

The parents insist police have determined their son's death was an accident based on poor police work. The child's mother, Elizabeth Carmichael, has refused to comment. An attorney spokesperson for the family supports their assertion that Alex Carmichael likely met with foul play. "The nature of the wounds is...indicative that he was injured in some fashion before he entered the water. The autopsy will reveal much more evidence to support our case."

Officer Barrick is reserving judgement, answering "No comment" to inquiries about the ongoing investigation. (Continued on page A-2)

School Closes
Brookings Elementary School will be closed early for the holidays as the staff and students mourn the loss of one of their own. "Alex was so nice," Natasha Milligan, a classmate, sobbed as school was closed down today. Alex Carmichael was a fifth grader at Brookings Elementary. School is expected to reopen January 3rd, 2008 as scheduled.

Of course, I remembered after I read this. I even remember Natasha crying like she was ever nice to or spent any time around Alex in school. He was in the other fifth grade class, so I didn't spend much time around him. Jesse and me barely knew him actually, but I remember him being a really quiet kid with dark hair and pale skin. He had these big brown eyes that always looked sad, and I always assumed it was because his family moved to way the hell over here from somewhere back East, I think it was. Jesse figured that maybe Alex's parents were right and he was killed, based on the answers he's given us to the questions. That one where he wrote "she kills" might not be what he wants me to do but something I am supposed to find out about. Jesse said he'd ask next time Alex comes around.

It was kind of fun in a terrible way, looking for all these clues like we were those meddling kids from the Scooby Doo cartoons. 'Cept usually there was some monster they were running from but in this case, I feel like I'm the monster.

January 14, 2014

Jesse managed to get a copy of the police and coroner's reports from his pal, Eric, whose dad is a deputy, by telling him it's for a paper he's writing about being a forensic investigator for his senior project. My man is super slick!

The report and the newspaper agree with each other; the police assumed Alex had gone walking along the ridge atop Haystack Rock and fallen in or been taken by surprise by the tide. The coroner said he was dead when he went in the water, from a blunt trauma to the head, likely from hitting the rocks on the way down. Jesse and me knew better.

January 17, 2014
Was by myself today, found this in my
notebook:

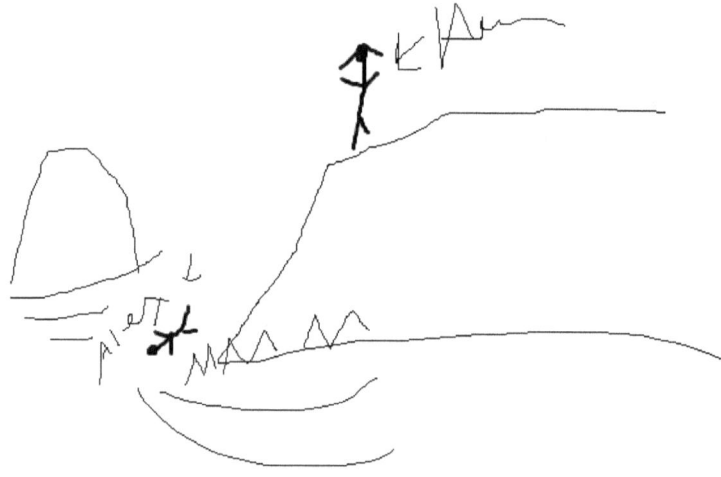

January 21, 2014

Another fun message from our friend Alex:

February 1, 2014
Alex left a message on my laptop. He typed it
this time, clever ghost. Er, kid. What the heck ever,
here's a copy and paste of his writing:
How can Eva help you?
Kill her
How did you die?
Dead in the water
Are you Alex Carmichael?

YES
Were you murdered?
Yes
Who killed you?
Her. Kill her

Not exactly Shakespeare. Basically he just typed some answers to the questions list, and not all of them, just these ones. I wish he'd be more specific! What am I supposed to do with that?

February 7, 2014

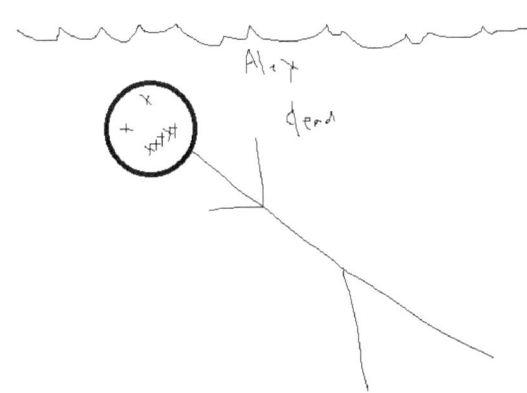

I know, Alex. I know.

February 14, 2014
We had the most romantic dinner together today, to celebrate our first Valentine's Day as a couple. When we were younger, of course, Valentine's Day was gross and for loser grown-ups and teenagers. We dressed nice and Jess picked me up in his mom's car instead of the drafty Jeep. We ate at the steakhouse outside of town because it's the nicest place around, unless you wanna drive clear into Eugene. I told Jesse I didn't care where we went as long as we were together. I then promptly made gagging and retching sounds at my own gaucherie,

on general principle. He responded by pinning me to the seat of the car and tickling me until I cried "uncle!" a million times. My hair was a wreck and I'm sure people in the restaurant thought we were making out in the car. I was probably beet red too! But not Jesse, that jerk.

Jesse bought me a special edition Coraline book signed by my favorite author! It's the best present I've ever gotten. I love him so much! I wish I'd thought of something better than that watch, but he said he liked it when we were in town shopping for our families during Christmas. I snuck back later with my mom and got it for him. He seemed to really like it but it's not as good as the book. Next time, I'll really wow him!

Things got pretty steamy after dinner. We were in the car, parked by the ocean; a perfect end to a perfect date. We talked about everything except Alex and spirit writing for a change, and after a while I slipped out of my seat belt and scooted closer to him. Jesse stopped us from going much farther than we already have though, which I was kind of disappointed about. I felt like he didn't want me anymore, maybe he was upset I didn't get him something better than the watch. But he said we had to stop, because our first time shouldn't be in a car, and that I deserved better than that.

He said, "The woman I love and the future mother of my children should have a perfect memory of her first time."

I admit it. I cried like a girl, and he held me close, stroking my hair, and then we talked about our future together and how many kids we would have. What we would name them when we would have them (after college, of course). He didn't say anything about being married but I don't care. I'll take every

92

part of his life he'll share with me.

He had gone from Eva's house after the last spirit-writing episode straight to Eric's house. Without giving away too many details about what Eva could do, Jesse convinced him to get copies of the Alex Carmichael case from his dad. They came up with a cover story about a senior project for school as the reason the documents were needed, and while they were confidential, Eric's old man didn't figure a cold case file would be of too much importance as long as they didn't use real names, he said.

Jesse showed the newspaper clipping he had found on file at the library to Eva and she remembered Alex right away. Alex had been the same age as Jesse and Natasha, and one year older than Eva.

"Oh my, God, Jesse! Do you think it's the same Alex Carmichael?"

"It has to be. Remember, when we asked how old he was, he said eleven, right? And his parents said he was killed all along but the cops never found anything to support that."

"The police report (nice job by the way) and the newspaper both say he fell and hit his head and then drowned. The drowned part is right, according to Alex."

Jesse frowned. "Alex's parents said he would have been able to swim to shore if he'd fallen in, but the blunt trauma part is plausible. Still, if he didn't have something to say about what happened to him, he wouldn't be communicating through you."

They'd left it at that for the moment. Until Alex came back, they had no more ideas how to get answers to their questions.

Then a couple days later, Alex wrote something in Eva's notebook, and then again a few days after that. Jesse was irrationally jealous. He seemed to remember Alex having a slight crush on Eva in grade school and now he felt weird about him using Eva's body to write messages. He knew it was crazy, but he couldn't help it. Jealous of a ghost!

Then Alex fired up the laptop, using Eva's hands, of course, and answered their questions. Well, sort of. He did confirm that he was in fact THE Alex Carmichael and that he had been murdered. He still didn't name his killer though.

Jesse decided it was too much for a while. He wanted some normalcy to come back to their lives, so he arranged a nice dinner for Valentine's Day. The twinkle of excitement in her eyes when she opened his gift, and the genuine gasp of surprise and happiness, when she saw that the book was signed by the author, made him want to bring that look to her face every single day. He loved watching her as he opened his gift, her uncertainty causing her to nibble on her lower lip in a way that was actually pretty sexy. After dinner, they drove around a while and then parked by their favorite wayside near the beach. They talked about school, their friends, anything other than Alex Carmichael or spirit writing. She told him about her dreams of becoming an author and illustrator of children's books, and he talked about photography and his dreams of taking the world's most recognized photos someday.

Naturally, as it seemed so often to happen these days, their talk turned to touch and that turned to fire. Jesse stopped it quickly though, knowing his control was wearing thin. He would be damned if their first time was in the car.

He told her that the future mother of his

children would have the most perfect memory of their first time making love, and she cried in his arms. He held her close, his eyes closed against his own tears that threatened to overwhelm him. After a time, they talked about their future. Where they would go to college. Where they would live. When to have kids, and how many, and what their names were going to be...no one said anything about spirit writing or the ghosts of dead boys.

Eva

February 15, 2013

I went to that doctor's appointment. Just in case. I was talking to Beth about it and Beth agreed to go with me for moral support, so we just went and the doctor asked questions that we giggled about later in Beth's room. I got the pill, and I started taking them this morning. Beth assured me that it's not a big deal. She has the pill too. We had girl talk about sex and boys, and did some female bonding. I feel like I have a best girlfriend for the first time in my life. I feel normal. It's indescribable.

February 16, 2013

My seventeenth birthday. Jesse's eighteenth birthday was September 3rd. I've never been happier, or felt freer. True, there's a dead kid from my past trying to tell me something but with Jesse by my side, even that feels like not really a huge deal. We'll get through it together.

I am the twisted and tangled of things,
rolled and unrolled from colorful skeins.
I am the master of this ship made of wings,
and I am the vessel which all of this brings.
Through my voice the wind howls and sings,
through my eyes see the splendor of rings.
Moonlight and sunlight by any means,
I am the creator of marvelous things.
I am the master of this ship made of words,
I am the owner of these thoughts never heard,
I am the lock whose door cannot open,
I am the key, which can never be broken.
My thoughts are the tangled and twisted of things,
Rolled and unrolled from bright colored skeins.

Imagination runs wild and rampant in me,
These are the things needing to be free.

February 25, 2014

I'm writing this after the fact. It's important that I record everything that has happened so I never forget how evil some people can be and also how there really are miracles, things that we can't explain away with coincidence. Magic, even the supernatural kind, should never be marginalized.

Justin showed up unexpectedly at my house on the 16th. He asked me to come to Haystack Rock because, he said, Natasha and Beth were there fighting, and Natasha had a knife. He said he didn't know what she was going to do and he seemed really scared.

Beth is my friend now; I didn't want her to get hurt by Natasha. I guess I also felt pretty guilty because it was pretty likely the reason they are fighting was because of me.

I told Justin I don't know what I can do, and he should probably do something. He's the guy after all, right? But he was useless, so I called him a pussy and made a huge mistake: I agreed to get in his car if he'd just get Natasha out of there as soon as I talked them into breaking it up.

In retrospect, this seems like the all time worst mistake that anyone has ever made in the history of the world. But I wasn't thinking about Alex or his dead broken body in the water at the base of Haystack Rock. I was thinking about how I couldn't bear it if Beth got hurt because she was a friend with me and Natasha was a crazy bitch.

Jesse got a message on his cell phone at work probably the same exact time I was getting into Justin's beat up Honda. It was from me, or at least

98

from my phone, though I'd left my cell phone on my computer desk like a complete idiot. The message said:

Hurry! I'm at Haystack Rock!

Jesse left Dutch Bros at a run, Eric said later. He didn't explain why, but Jesse said to me privately that he was afraid I went there to try to talk to Alex on my own, or force him to write something useful. He said he was sure I was having an "episode" and was worried that anything might happen to me in that state. He didn't dream I'd do something as reckless as going anywhere with Justin. I'm still in a lot of trouble all the way around on that one.

Jesse had called 911 on his way to the beach and then raced along the deserted cliffs, looking for me. He found me, too, trapped out on Haystack Rock with Natasha, Justin, and two of his friends whose names I can't remember. They were holding me down while Justin was cutting off my clothes. He saw Jesse coming and told him if he came any closer, he'd cut off my tit. I guess he wanted to show Jess he meant business because he sliced me right open under my right boob along my rib cage. The pain was intense and immediate. I screamed and one of Justin's thug friends hit me with his closed fist in the mouth. It kind of made me pass out, or gray out a little.

Jesse told me later that I appeared to be "in" my body, because I was screaming and writhing; my eyes were wild but lucid, he said. I remember none of that, but I do remember suddenly hearing his tense voice saying that the tide was coming in, which will cover the land bridge that connects Haystack Rock to the cliff side. He screamed for Natasha to tell her dogs to let me go, but she just laughed at him. It was the most brittle sound I've ever heard a human make, like broken glass in people form. She asked why he couldn't just be happy with her. "No one is EVER happy with me! No matter what I do, how much I put out, or how tough I am, no one ever picks me!" she had screamed.

I was still on the ground, Justin held his knife over me and his thugs held down my arms and legs. I heard Jesse tell Natasha that he was sorry that her family was so awful to her, that her daddy only paid attention to her sister and her stepbrother molested her, but that was no reason to hurt Eva.

She screamed and cursed at him, told him he was no better than that stupid Alex kid who refused to believe her when she told him what was happening to her, and how he had rejected her.

Jesse

Jesse showed up to work on the 16th early, wanting to leave early so he could get to the store for some flowers. Today was Eva's seventeenth birthday, and he'd planned to propose to her. A couple days before, he had gone to her dad's classroom during his prep period and asked for his permission to marry his daughter. Mr. D had seemed a little taken aback, because he said, "What? Now?"

"No sir, after college. But I wanted to propose to her on her birthday so she would know how I feel about her and that I will wait for her to finish high school so we can go to college together."

"Well, well. I can't say I'm surprised. You and Eva together have always made sense. I was concerned there for a while."

"Yes, sir, I understand. But I was just a kid..."

"I know, Jesse, it wasn't a criticism, just an observation. I'm a science teacher, it's what I do."

Jesse laughed dutifully, but waited for Mr. Dunbar to answer. Finally he let up.

"Of course, you have my blessing, provided you both wait until after college to get married and have kids. Ok?"

"Yes, sir!"

Jesse was elated. On the morning of her birthday, he'd asked his mom to have his grandmother's ring cleaned and polished. Then he had told her about his plans to ask Eva to marry him. She had gone to her room without saying anything. When she came back, she had a red leather box in her hand. She held it out to him; her eyes gleaming with unshed tears.

"It was your grandmother's. She wanted your

wife to have it."

Jesse opened the box. Inside was an enormous, solitaire diamond encased in a filigree setting, sparkling brightly in the dull light of the kitchen's bulb. He hugged his mother tightly, unable to form the words of gratitude stuck in his throat.

Halfway through his shift, his phone buzzed in his pocket. He finished the drink he was making and thanked the customer at the drive through. Pulling his phone out of his pocket, he saw it was a text from Eva, saying to hurry she was at Haystack Rock.

What the hell was she doing there? How did she get there? He didn't know but he didn't like it. He called to Eric to cover for him and ran for the Jeep. What if she was trying to make an episode happen, with no one there? Shit. He slammed the Jeep into gear and raced for the part of the beach where Haystack Rock was accessible at low tide. Wrestling his phone from his pocket, he dialed 9-1-1 and yelled at the dispatcher to send someone to the beach immediately. He hung up and flung the phone into the passenger seat, breaking several speed laws on the way. He parked sideways in the wayside parking lot and launched himself from the vehicle, racing for the cliffs.

Out on the promontory of Haystack Rock, Jesse saw something that made him weak all over. For a moment he thought he might actually puke. Eva was out there, pinned to the ground by two guys Jesse knew as Justin's friends, while Justin himself was cutting off Eva's clothes. Justin saw Jesse coming closer and screamed at him.

"Don't come any closer fuckhead, or I'll cut her tits off!"

To punctuate his sincerity, Justin placed the flat of the knife under Eva's right breast and drew a deep red line across her flesh. Jesse cried out in horror. Eva screamed in pain, and one of Justin's cronies punched her in the mouth. She went limp, and Jesse saw red.

"The fucking tide is coming in, Natasha," he shouted. "Tell Justin and his fuck buddies to let Eva go, NOW!"

Jesse saw Natasha's red lips curl in evil laughter, her blond hair whipping across her face in the wind, swept up by the tide. She screamed at him, cursing his name, crying that no one ever chose her.

"I'm sorry no one is nice to you at home, Natasha. I really am. I wish your stepfather and your mother listened to you when you told them your stepbrother was molesting you. But Eva didn't do any of that to you, you know that. Come on. Just let her go, and I'll help you..."

"FUCK YOU, JESSE! You think I don't know you'll just ignore me again? That's what guys do right? Unless my legs are spread you don't give a SHIT about me! None of you do! You think this jackass likes me?" she pointed at Justin, who had the nerve to look a little wounded about being called a jackass. "NO! He only likes me for the booze I can get from my stepdad's liquor cabinet and for the head I give him in his shitty basement. He doesn't care about me AT ALL! Just like that stupid fuck, Alex, didn't care about me in grade school. He said he would tell everyone what he saw me doing with the junior high boys. I told him that my stepbrother made me do it, but HE DIDN'T BELIEVE ME! He would have told EVERYONE! And my mom would have sent me away! Then they could have their PERFECT FUCKING FAMILY without poor messed up Natasha fucking everything up for them!"

She turned to Justin, her make up running in

streams down her face, his Mohawk a sad thing in the driving mist of the ocean breaking around them as the tide came in, whipped to fury by the wind. "THROW THAT FUCKING BITCH IN!" Natasha screamed at him, nearly doubled over with the force of her own voice.

Eva

I saw Natasha turn, her mascara running down her cheeks and her perfect hair tossed by the windy ocean air. She shrieked at Justin to throw the little bitch into the water. It took me a minute to figure out that the bitch was me.

They hesitated, probably because Jesse was there to witness it, and she freaked the hell out. She was screaming all sorts of obscene words, asking how I liked knowing that my boyfriend was thinking of her while he screwed me, and other awful things I will never be able to unhear. She strode over to me and pulled me up by the hair, yanking me to my feet and trying to push me over the far edge of Haystack Rock, away from Jesse.

Jesse leapt over the nearly covered narrow strip of connecting land and punched both Justin's henchmen out cold. I didn't get to see this but I wish he'd had time to kick them in the ribs. The things they had told me they were going to do to me will haunt my nightmares for the rest of my life.

Justin ducked and ran, jumping across to safety and getting in his car just in time for the cops to show up and arrest him. I missed that part, too, but I was seriously hoping there would be an episode of "Cops" to record the whole thing. Unfortunately, there was not.

The other cops ran out to Haystack Rock in time to see Natasha lose her footing and fall off the rock, holding on to my hair. I remember screaming, the intense pain, and the sight of Jesse lunging for me.

I remember falling off the edge of the rocks and that sickening feeling in my stomach, like the bottom of an elevator dropping out from underneath me, and loud shrieking that I thought was me. The pain in my scalp abruptly stopped, reduced to a dull throb all over my head. I remember hanging there and my fingers hurting like hell and feeling a giant weight hanging off of me and I saw Jesse grab my hands, trying to pull me up, shouting, "Don't look down, Eva!" over and over so, of course, I looked down. I saw Natasha hanging off of my pants and she was the one making all the noise, screaming and trying to climb up me, digging her nails into my skin under my jeans and she grabbed my hair again, pinching and pulling and twisting so I punched her, over and over. I remember that my fist hit her nose with a horrible crunching sound, like the sound your teeth make when biting through celery with peanut butter, which I will never be able to eat again, and she fell, she fell because of me. Fell down, such a long ways, her body twisting over and over, screaming, such an impossibly long way down. Later the coroner said that the fall on the jagged rocks alone would have killed her, but the strong riptide had pulled her under and finished the job.

I must have closed my eyes; the next thing I can remember is the feeling of being carried and I cracked my eyes open a tiny bit. I could see/hear/smell/feel Jesse carrying me, his scent of Axe deodorant and hair gel mixing with that smell of just Jesse, a male scent that never fails to make me dizzy. I could hear his heart beating like a giant drum next to my ear, my head resting on his broad chest, and I could see the soft blue material of my favorite sweatshirt of his. It's a baby blue color, worn and washed so many times that the cloth is thin, molding to his body and smelling like him no matter if it's fresh from the dryer at his parents' house or not. I was planning to steal it, and I was outraged to see he'd spilled red paint all over the front of it. I opened my mouth to yell at him but then I don't remember anything coming out. He told me later at the hospital that all that red paint was my blood from the wounds Natasha had given me, pulling out hunks of my hair. The worst was the knife wound from Justin; I'll always have a scar under my right boob. There goes my bikini-modeling career.

Then I'm lying down and seeing Jesse's face looming over mine. He was saying something over and over again but my ears weren't working so I don't know what it was. It looked like he was saying "I love you" but I can't be sure. Everything was so fuzzy, and bright at the same time; it made him have a halo around his blond hair and I almost giggled. My angel, I remember thinking, knowing all the times we had seriously made out and almost went too far made him less than an angel. Me too, I guess.

Justin hesitated to throw Eva in the water, and Natasha lost her mind. Screaming obscene shit at everyone, she ran over to where Eva lay on the ground bleeding and yanked her to her feet by her hair, pushing her to the edge of the cliff. Jesse bellowed in anger and rushed them, punching first one of Justin's friends and then the other. Both of them went down like a sack of rocks. Justin ran, ducking Jesse's wild swing, and booked it for the wayside parking lot. Just in time, too, for the cops to show up and throw his ass in handcuffs.

On the rock, Natasha and Eva went over the edge of the cliff in front of Jesse's eyes. He screamed in pain, and fear and grief, lunging to the edge and throwing himself flat, unable to look and see Eva's shattered body below but unable not to look. He saw her though, her small strong fingers clutching the sturdy coastal grasses that covered the rocks and sand, Natasha clinging to her, her hands grabbing Eva's dark hair and trying to pull her down the cliff, intent on Eva's death and impervious to her own.

"Don't look down, Eva!" he shouted and she looked up at him, her eyes enormous, eating up her face. He grabbed her hands, trying to pull her up. Natasha began screaming at him, at Eva, cursing and pinching Eva, pulling her hair, doing anything she could to hurt her and make her lose her grip on Jesse.

Jesse saw Eva double up her fist before she pulled it from his grasp. She turned slightly, her left hand gripping him so tightly his hand hurt for days afterward, and her left fist punching Natasha in the face over and over until her nose broke, and blood gushed everywhere. Natasha howled in pain and let go of Eva, falling over and over down the face of Haystack Rock until her body landed on the sharp jagged rocks below. Jesse saw her broken body in the foamy waves, her blood leaking from her and staining the water at the base of the rock, her blue eyes open to the heavens, staring at nothing.

Jesse wrenched his eyes from Natasha's dead body and concentrated on the woman he loved. He pulled her up, her body limp and unresponsive. He knelt by her, frantically seeking a pulse. A police officer approached him cautiously, glancing over the cliff side at the torn body of Natasha before coming back to Jesse.

"Is she breathing son?"

"I don't know, I don't know!"

"Let me check her, ok?"

"NO! I will do it!"

"You're not doing her any favors son. Let me check her and then you can have her back, ok?"

Jesse nodded but didn't move. The officer leaned down and checked Eva's vital signs. She was breathing shallowly, her pulse erratic. "She's lost a lot of blood. Let's get her to the ambulance."

Jesse picked Eva up in his arms, her blood staining his shirt immediately, shaking his head at the offer of assistance from the officers now swarming Haystack Rock. The young officer who had first approached him followed him all the way to the waiting ambulance, past the patrol car where Justin Perkins and his henchmen were cuffed and waiting their ride down to the jail.

He laid her gently on the gurney, and clambered into the ambulance with her. There was no question that he was going to the hospital with her. It was unnerving though, to hear the paramedics call out her waning vital signs in their lingo. Her blood pressure tanked, and he saw them exchanging worried glances before applying oxygen and setting up the IV line.

Jesse broke down quietly in the corner of the ambulance, staying out of their way but watching her face for any sign of life. He swore he could see her growing paler and paler, and knew he was watching her die before his eyes.

Eva

When I next came around, I was standing in a room, light headed and dizzy. There were a bunch of doctors standing around body on a blue draped table, all of them wearing those green masks that make them look as if they are trying to avoid the plague. I could see the blue, green, hazel, and brown glints in their eyes above those masks, each one saying something with their heavy glances but in an eye language I couldn't decipher.

I felt a warm hand slip into mine, and I looked over to see a young boy, about twelve or so, with deep, rich brown hair and chocolate eyes taking in the scene of all those doctors clustered around the person on the blue table. I couldn't believe I was finally seeing him after these last couple of months of torment.

"Alex?"

He smiled at me. I noticed how long and dark his eyelashes were, and how there were a slight constellation of freckles spread across the milky way of his nose. He was the most wonderful looking boy I'd ever seen. I felt the warmth of his hand spread along my hand and fingers, up my arm, and infusing me with heat, like the comfort of a fire in the hearth after being outside on a chilly winter's day.

"Hey, Eva. Bad day, huh?" His voice was raspy, like he hadn't used it in a long time, and sounded older than the young face that accompanied it.

"That's kind of unclear right now. That's me on the table, though isn't it?"

He nodded. I'd known, of course, but his confirmation was disheartening. I wasn't ready to die.

"What's it like?"

"It's not so bad, really. I want to thank you, though. If you and Jesse hadn't listened to me, I'd still be stuck here. Now I can go...wherever's next."

"Am I supposed to go with you?"

He didn't say anything for a minute. Then, "Well, that's really up to you, but what about Jesse? You guys have been meant for each other since we were kids."

"You're still a kid," I smirked at the dead boy. He grinned, aw shucks, at me and squeezed my hand. "I want to go back. How do I do that?"

"I can send you back, if you really want to. It's going to hurt a lot, but I think it will be worth it, later," was his reply.

"Oh yeah? And what do you know about it?"

Again, I got that shy, smirky grin from him. It faded quickly, though, and he leaned toward me, closer and closer, until his lips hovered over mine and he said, "I've wanted to do this since third grade," and he kissed me. For a brief moment, I was too surprised to react, and then I thought about Jesse; I guess this wasn't technically cheating since Alex was dead, but I didn't feel the same as I did when Jesse and me kissed. Still, it was sort of sweet.

"Thank you, Eva," he breathed when the kiss ended. And then he blew, gently, into my face and I smelled the antiseptic odor of a sterilized environment and the body on the bed, my body, gasped as the doctors shouted amongst themselves. I glanced over; they'd pulled out those paddle thingies and were shocking the hell out of me, making my body dance on the bed like a marionette. I looked frantically back at the now fading form of Alex, the boy who had been stuck dead in the water.

"Don't worry, Eva. Everything's gonna be ok.

But don't tell Jesse I kissed you; he'll be super pissed," Alex grinned as he said it.

I wanted to ask him. You know, ask him what it was like, if there was anything after, worth looking forward to? But I didn't.

"Hey Alex? Thanks for talking to me. And by the way, you can't draw for shit."

The last thing I felt was a final squeeze of his warm hand, and then he let me go and I felt nothing. I heard an echo in my head of a young boy's carefree laugh, and then silence. The next thing I remember, I woke up in my white hospital bed, bristling with wires and tubes, to find Jesse asleep in the chair next to me. His tall body was folded up in the chair like origami and I wondered sort of faintly if he'd been there long. He wasn't going to be able to walk, if so.

I found out when Jesse woke up to me whispering his name that Justin and his friends were sent to jail. Well, mostly what I got when I woke Jesse up was his strong arms and his soft lips but we set the monitors off, beeping and screaming everywhere and scaring the bejeesus out of us. Fortunately, we were fast enough for him to get outta my bed and back in his seat before the nurse came in. All she saw was us holding hands. She kinda raised her eyebrow a little bit but didn't say anything, other than it was nice to have me back.

Anyway, after she left to get me some juice, I asked Jess to tell me what happened while I was out. Evidently, Natasha Milligan had been hanging out with Justin Perkins and all his friends, giving them sexual favors and doing drugs with them, paying for everything. She tried to get them to kill me so she could have Jesse back, by drowning me in the ocean like she did to Alex Carmichael. They agreed if she agreed to let them use me anyway they wanted; she was enraged that they wanted me instead of her and then decided that it didn't matter as long as she got Jesse back.

Jesse

At the hospital, the paramedics wheeled the gurney containing the body of the girl he loved rapidly down the hallway to the ER triage room. He followed, unnoticed, until the blue drapes came out to cover her body while the surgeons closed her wound and began blood transfusions. A doctor came to him.

"Say something to her, she may be able to hear you. It might matter to you, later, that you did." There was no time to sugar coat it.

He leaned over her, kissed her lips, and told her he loved her over and over until they took her away and left him there, the only physical sign of her existence staining the blue of his sweatshirt. Jesse sank to the floor, his mind blank. He couldn't fathom a life without Eva.

He made his way to the small waiting room of Brookings Hospital. After a few minutes, one of the nurses came through on her rounds and found him curled in a ball in the corner of the room.

"Oh honey. Come here," she said sympathetically. Jesse didn't move, so she came to him and wrapped her arms around him. "You have people you want me to call, Hon?"

He handed her his phone. She dialed the one labeled, "Home" and got his mom on the line. She called his father at work, and they both went to the high school to be with Eva's parents when they arrived at the hospital.

Two hours later, the doctor came in to the waiting room where Jesse, his family, and Eva's parents all waited for news of their beloved girl. He spoke quietly and frankly.

"It was very close. Her heart stopped once on

the operating table for about three minutes, but we were able to restart her heart. She is in stable condition now, and received a massive transfusion. She's a lucky young lady. She's lost a great deal of blood, but I think she will make a full recovery. There will be a scar on her torso, but I know a plastic surgeon that can help when the time comes. You may all go in and see her, one at a time, and it's best if someone is here when she wakes up."

"Thank you, doctor," Eva's mother said, her chin quivering but her voice firm. Eva's father cried quietly behind his wife, his hand on her shoulder. Jesse's parents held each other close, their eyes shining with sympathy for their friends.

"Thank goodness she's ok," Jesse's father said.

"Thank goodness for Jesse," Eva's mother responded. She crossed the room to where Jesse sat hunched in a chair, his mind still in shock that Eva was alive. "You saved her, Jesse, in more ways than one. Thank you so much for saving my daughter."

She placed her hands on either side of his face and kissed his forehead. One by one, the parents left the room to go and see Eva. It was unspoken but agreed that Jesse would be staying at the hospital. He followed them slowly, Jesse's dad let him know he would come back and bring Jesse some clothes. The nurse had found a scrub top that fit him, but his clothes still bore traces of the day's events. He nodded, not trusting himself to speak.

Finally, after a long time, all the adults left. Jesse's dad had come and gone with the clothes, clapping a hand on his son's shoulder in sympathy on the way out. Jesse was finally alone with Eva.

She lay in the hospital bed, eyes closed and tubes running into her veins under the covers. A cannula was attached to her face, forcing oxygen into her nose and lungs and machines beeped quietly, measuring her vital signs with reassuring regularity.

Jesse sat in the chair next to her bed, his hand holding her still one under the covers. He was so grateful she was alive; he didn't think he could find the words. Finally, he just started talking.

"Christ, Eva, what the hell were you thinking, going out there with that scumbag? I can't believe you did that. Actually, I can believe it. You're never afraid of anything. It's always been like that. Remember when we were kids, and I wouldn't swim in the ocean because I was afraid of sharks? Remember what you told me? You said, 'Better to be eaten by sharks than die a coward,' and you were only like eight years old then. And so I went swimming with you, and we didn't get eaten by sharks. You were always bold like that, but you were right. I don't know what I would ever do without you. I'd never chance anything; never try anything new or dangerous. Don't ever leave me, Eva. I'll die if you do."

He cried for a while, finally giving in to exhaustion and curling up in the chair as best he could, vowing to be the first thing she saw when she woke up and the last thing he saw when he fell asleep was her beautiful, sleeping face.

And that was how it happened. Jesse woke to an angel whispering his name. He sprang from the chair, his back protesting the long hours twisted into unnatural shapes, and wrapped her in his arms, squeezing her tight and vowing over and over to never let her go. He spoke rapidly, making promises to always be there for her, to always protect her until she stopped him with a kiss. He nearly climbed into the bed with her, wanting nothing more than to be as close to her as humanly possible, but the machines she was hooked up to started beeping alarm signals and he returned to his chair just before the nurse came in.

"Good, you're awake. Nice to have you back Eva. I thought this guy here was going to need a bed of his own, you nearly drove him out of his mind. I'll go get the doctor, but can I bring you anything while you're waiting?"

Eva asked for some juice and the nurse left. She turned to Jesse. "Ok, tell me what happened. Did that asshole, Justin, get a new roommate in jail? You know, the kind they call Bubba?"

Jesse laughed a little. It was going to take a while to bring back that carefree feeling he'd had before Eva was nearly killed. He concentrated on telling her the story without bringing back any of the fear she must have felt when they were trying to kill her.

"We saw Natasha had been hanging out with Justin after you and I got together, right?" She nodded. "So I guess she was doing sexual favors for all three of them; Justin, and his two buddies, Isaac Reyes, and John Ficken. Ficken was the dude who punched you," he added, seeing a fierce expression come over her at the mention of Justin's friends.

"Anyway, she was stealing money from her mother to pay for their drugs, and stealing alcohol from her stepfather's liquor cabinet to give those guys. She started talking to them when they were drugged up and drunk, giving them, uh, you know sexual things while they were messed up. She was telling them how I was such a jerk and how you were, um, a slut, and that if they helped her get rid of you, then she could have me back. I guess Justin didn't care about her that much because he agreed to do it if they could uh, well, have you. You know, before they killed

118

you. I guess that pissed her off but she decided it didn't matter if she could have me. I don't imagine my opinion on the matter was taken into consideration, let alone yours."

"Those fuckers," Eva growled. Jesse chuckled. She was such a fighter.

"So...long story short, Justin spilled the whole story and made Natasha the mastermind of the whole thing. One thing he said was that her stepbrother, Mark, was um, molesting her, and finally there will be an investigation into what really went on in that house. Not that it does her much good now," he added a little sadly. He felt sorry for Natasha, but not sorry enough to dismiss the fact she'd tried to kill Eva.

"You could have died," he said softly.

She looked at him intently. "But I didn't."

"No, you didn't."

Jesse didn't tell her about the doctor saying her heart had stopped on the operating table for three minutes. And she didn't bring it up again. Finally, the doctor came in and unhooked her from some of the machines. The nurse didn't say anything, but she did bring Eva's juice and an extra pillow, handing it to Jesse with a raised eyebrow. He smiled his best Jesse Williams, megawatt grin at her and she chuckled, exiting the room and leaving them alone.

He climbed up in the bed with Eva, taking care not to jostle her or mess with her IV tubes. He pulled her small body close to his and wrapped himself around her. She sighed in contentment. "It was a long day, wasn't it babe?"

He snorted. "Yeah something like that. Go to sleep, sweetheart."

She did. So did he.

Eva

March 14, 2014

I was in the hospital for two weeks. I guess when you almost die, they want to make sure you're ok before they let you go. You know, so they can't get in trouble if you croak in their driveway or something.

Anyway, Jess visited me every day, and my parents and his parents too. Eric and Beth visited a few times, which was super sweet. Eric told me I wasn't allowed to die right when Jesse finally got a normal girlfriend. Me! NORMAL? That was so awesome of Eric to say. I almost hugged him. I did hug Beth though. Carefully, I was still all scarred up and it hurt like a bitch most of the time. She promised to take me shopping when I got better, and honestly I can say I was really looking forward to it.

When I got home, my notebook was open and Alex had written, "Thank you" in it. I showed it to Jesse and he told me about Alex using my phone to text message him that I was in trouble. We checked our phones, to have these mementos of him more than anything, but they were gone from both our phones. Oh well. At least it's over and Alex can go peacefully wherever he was supposed to go next. We held each other a while and then things heated up as they usually do but I was scared. What if he didn't want to touch me with the scar? What if he felt like I was, I dunno, no good anymore because of what those guys were planning to do?

Jesse

It took Eva a long time to recover, a lot longer than Jesse had imagined. The wound on her side was ugly, red and puffy, and stayed that way for many weeks. The stitches looked as though they were going to pull out of her flesh, and she made jokes about being Frankenstein's monster, but he knew it bothered her.

One night in April, an unseasonably warm day spurred them to the beach, far from Haystack Rock, where Jesse pulled his new blue hoodie over his head and dropped it in the Jeep's driver seat. Eva was wearing a white tank top under her hoodie and refused to take her sweater off, knowing her scar would be visible through the thin fabric of the tank top.

"Come on, babe, it's fine. No one is going to notice and fuck 'em if they do," he coaxed.

Finally, the worst happened. Eva started crying. He grabbed her and pulled her to him, and she fought him as always. "Why? Why did this happen to me? I didn't ask for any of it. ANY OF IT!" she sobbed into his chest, hitting him with her small fists over and over until he caught her fists in one hand and held them behind her.

Jesse stroked her hair with his free hand and murmured soothing words. Finally, her tears tapered off to occasional hiccups and she pushed away from him. He released her hands and she glared up at him. "Sorry," she muttered. He didn't say anything. He took a step toward her and she held her ground, her stance defiant. He kissed her soft lips once, twice, and again until she responded, her body language cooling off from anger to desire, in spite of herself. With a swift movement that caught her breath in her throat, he pulled her hoodie up over her head and tossed it into the Jeep. The tops of her perky breasts peeked at him at the neck of her tank top, and her slender figure was emphasized by its clingy fabric. He let his eyes roam over her. Her cheeks were flushed and her eyes bright. He didn't notice any scar. All he saw was her beauty.

"You're amazing," he said softly. "Desirable. Hot. Mine."

He swept her up in his arms, careful not to pull on the injured side, and carried her down to the beach. Finally, she laughed, released from her hang-up about the scar. She had Jesse. She didn't need anyone else's opinion. They spent the day frolicking in the waves and laughing, playing tag and wrestling gently in the sand. She drew huge hearts in the wet sand with their initials in them, and he lay in the dry sand, sprawled full length and one hand propping up his head, watching the woman he loved play with the ocean.

He still waited for the right moment to propose to her, but knew she was still too fragile. Her outburst at the Jeep had proven that. She told him a little bit about what Justin and his buddies had said they were going to do to her and he could tell she was conflicted about her own desires now. He kind of thought maybe she was worried about his feelings for her after everything that happened, but he hoped not. He did everything he could to let her know how much he desired her still, how much he loved her. He knew she still wanted him, could tell when he kissed her. She responded as always, but then pulled back after a few minutes. Before, he was the one who had stopped them but nowadays he didn't even have a chance. He only hoped time would heal her wounds, both the ones on the outside and the ones on the inside.

Eva

April 16, 2014

Jesse and I have been pretty busy. Since February, when Natasha Milligan and her friends tried to kill me, a lot has happened. First of all, Justin Perkins went to prison for attempted first-degree murder. Since he was a senior, and eighteen, he was, of course, tried as an adult. His two pals were also sentenced but they got lighter sentences, accessory to attempted murder. In any case, they won't be bugging us for a while.

We had to testify against them though, that was awful. I had to say in court the vile things they'd told me they were going to do to me. Jesse held my hand the whole time and seemed really calm, but I could tell he was mega pissed. I'd never told him exactly what they said and I'm not gonna write it here so I can look back and dwell on it. It was bad, end of story.

One of the hardest things to deal with has been my scar. It didn't heal very well. I was really self-conscious about it for a long time, until Jesse finally tore my hoodie off my body and let me know in no uncertain terms that he still thought I was sexy. I had been kinda holding back from him until he did that. I was sure he'd want to find a new girl who wasn't all scarred up and a freak to boot. I guess I was wrong. Thank God.

May 4, 2014

Today is the best day of my life. Last night,

Jesse and I had a bonfire on the beach, just the two of us. We had a picnic dinner and watched the sun set. It was totally cliché and cheesy and perfect. Just as the sun hit the water on the horizon's edge, Jess turned to me and kissed me and let me tell you it was the best kiss yet.

And then he said it. "Eva Dunbar, will you marry me??? I mean, you know, when we grow up?"

And I cried and blubbered, "yes."

He put the most amazing ring with a big honking diamond on my finger and I might have thrown myself at him. We'll worry about the details later, where to live, where to go to college, when to have kids...none of that mattered in that moment.

We finally sealed our bond in the time-honored way, in the sand with the ocean's waves urging us on. Jesse was so good to me, and I was so ready. I felt no pain, like other girls do, but only pleasure and he buried his face in my neck whispering my name over and over at the end. I'll never forget it as long as I live.

June 23, 2014

I haven't had any episodes of spirit writing since the last time Alex contacted me. Jesse says it's because I was under anesthetic and it ruined my psychic mojo or connection in my brain or some scientific-y crap. God I love him. I'm guessing it has something to do with us consummating our relationship (I've always wanted to use that word in a sentence).

I decided to stop writing this journal. There isn't anything weird about me to write down anymore. I'm just your average happiest girl on earth.

Alex Carmichael watched Eva grow into a self-assured young woman, with Jesse at her side. He saw her struggles and triumphs, and was proud of her when she graduated, first in high school as valedictorian, and then did the same in college, with honors.

He oversaw their lives, constantly checking in on them and making sure everything was going according to plan. The plan he'd have had if he had lived, for himself, or for her.

He was grateful for the man Jesse became and how he stood by Eva's side through their lives together, raising three beautiful children and loving each other madly, deeply.

And he waited for them, in his little-boy form, waited patiently for them to come play in the ocean's gentle waves with him, to let the water lap over their feet and to dig their toes in the sand, laughing. Always laughing.

About the Author:

Chrystal (Christina) Vaughan (1976-present) is the author of Dead in the Water, a paranormal young adult novel. Mrs. Vaughan lives in the Pacific Northwest with her husband and two daughters. When she is not writing or teaching, she is an avid reader and enjoys spinning yarn. She is currently at work on other novels, as well as a children's book.

Acknowledgements:

Thanks to my husband for putting up with ink stains on his coffee cups and the nightlight on during odd hours. Also, thank you to my children (biological and otherwise) for their continued enthusiasm and support. Thanks to my proofreader, Dee van der Vyver, and my editor, Kathy Mehl, and my test readers, Kymri Butcher, Dayna Clark, Laura Nolte, and Heather Tramp. You guys rock!

Social Media Links:

Facebook:
https://www.facebook.com/chrystalwrites

Twitter: https://twitter.com/TheChrystalShip

Blog: http://chrystalvaughan.blogspot.com

Pinterest:
http://www.pinterest.com/chrystalvaughn/